Project Manticore

Ryan A. Bunting

Copyright

Disclaimer

Project Manticore's story and characters are fictitious. Certain institutions, agencies, and public offices are mentioned, and quotations from real people are used for effect, but the characters involved and the events that take place are wholly imaginary. Any similarity in name or demeanor is purely coincidental.

Table of Contents

Dedication

This book is dedicated to my wife Patricia and to my late father Eugene. You both encouraged my dark sense of humor, and you both encouraged me to be my entire self without any scruples. For that I will never be able to thank you enough, but I figured a book dedication was probably a good start.

Chapter 1 - The Prisoners

The rain pattered loudly on the railings, resonating with a twang on the metallic deck as the ship rocked violently in the storm. A faint light in the distance let them know they were close.

"20 minutes to arrival!" shouted a guard towards the bow of the ship. "Strap yourselves in for berthing!"

Joseph Marquez was already strapped in, hand and foot - in fetters.

"Marquez... what do you think this shit is all about?" said Miller, rattling his chains.

"I don't know, but I don't think they're giving us the entire story. Nobody knows what goes on at Petty Island, all we know is what they tell us," Marquez whispered. He glanced back out to the dark waters of the Delaware River for a time.

The rain began to slow, and the suits on the guards began to shine with the light of the dock. The reflections on the water danced as the boat drifted towards the berth.

"Round up the prisoners and bring them on shore. Get them cleaned up and brought up to operations for briefing," an unknown voice said on a large radio tower sitting mid ship.

A group of guards approached the prisoners and gestured for them to get on their feet. The guards positioned the captives in single file and began marching them along the slender plank to the dock, the metallic scraping of the chains along the gangplank resonated in the eerily quiet darkness. The shoreline quickly turned into a tree line, but the red hue of lighting bled through the trees, pointing the way to the operations center.

"This is it huh?" whispered Miller.

"Be quiet!" the guard seethed.

The guards and prisoners proceeded up a metal staircase to the second-floor catwalk of the edifice. Another guard was waiting with an open door as the line piled in. The prisoners saw benches and lockers in the flickering fluorescent lighting, with fresh uniforms for soldiers in the DRA Army.

"What the fuck is this? I did my time in the army three years ago, what kind of prison sentence is this?" one of the prisoners said.

"The Democratic Republic of the Americas is a just and forgiving nation. The commander will fill you in with the details later. For now, enjoy the clean, dry clothing we have graciously supplied you with."

Marquez and Miller looked at each other with pained, shallow expressions. They were quickly reminded of a time they wished to forget.

"Never thought we'd be wearing these things again, eh?" Marquez quipped, trying to lighten the mood. Miller stared at the uniform with nervous hesitation. He ran his fingers along the shoulder pads, black as the sea they just arrived on. The helmet's subtle glow from the heads-up display on the visor. He didn't want to be that man again, and neither did Marquez.

"Let's just get this over with and find out what the fuck is going on here," Miller said curtly.

The prisoners were all suited up, sitting on the benches in the flickering room. Clad in black armored suits, their eyes glowing from the HUD projectors on their visors. Many of the prisoners had their visors raised, as many people didn't like the way the respirators feel inside the helmet. All citizens were required to do two years of "Volunteer National Defense" for the DRA military, so the suits were familiar - though not in a pleasant way - to everyone in the room.

"Yo fellas! There's some smokes in here!" one of the prisoners remarked excitedly, upon finding a fresh pack of cigarettes in one of the lockers. Some of the prisoners didn't partake, but Miller gladly accepted. The blue of the butane turned the tip of the cigarette a glowing crimson orange. The wisps of smoke gently twirled from the tip as he took a deep breath. He sighed the fire from his lungs, getting just a little of the weight off of his shoulders. He looked over to Marquez and offered him the lit cigarette.

Marquez hesitated for a second, but ultimately relented. "Fuck it, we were going to die anyway if we didn't sign up for this bullshit. Might as well have a vice before we inevitably die on fucking Petty Island of all places."

"Maybe we'll finally find out what they've been doing here at least," Miller responded sarcastically.

"Pfft, yeah right. We got 10 lashes for even bringing it up during boot camp," one of the prisoners scoffed.

The sound of the guards' boots clanking rhythmically on the steps disrupted their conversation.

"Gentlemen, if you'll come with me please."

The prisoners formed a line, just like when they were enlisted, and followed the guard up the next set of stairs to the briefing room of the command center. The room was surrounded by glass on three sides, overlooking the forest on the other side of a large wall, with spotlights showing a brief glimpse into the wooded area beyond. The rain droplets shimmered in the beams of light emitting from the spotlights, but the first thing anyone noticed were the mounted guns on the wall.

"Why are those guns facing inwards?" one of the prisoners remarked.

"Hmm, it seems your time out of the military hasn't made you completely soft. Keen observation," the commander said without looking up. The commander was sitting at a large oak desk. The screen embedded beneath the surface had an overview of the layout of the island on it, which he was looking at intently.

"What's this all about?" Miller piped in, feeling more courageous now that someone else had already spoken out of turn. Marquez shot him a look that, without saying a word, conveyed a message to the effect of *"what the fuck?"*

The commander finally looked up, "You're about to find out." The commander slid open a drawer in his desk and pulled out a slim cigar. He cut the tip and struck a match, taking three small, deliberate puffs.

"First, allow me to introduce myself. I'm Commander Wilkins, and welcome to Petty Island. Gentlemen, would you be so kind as to extend the same courtesy?"

"Henry Miller."

"Joseph Marquez, sir."

"Philip Waters."

"Andrew Feig."

"Thank you, now, onto what you're here for. Henry Miller and Joseph Marquez, theft of rations at Rose Cross Military Base in Philadelphia, Pennsylvania. Sentenced to death, commuted to special service. Philip Waters and Andrew Feig, spreading anti-government propaganda, and on non-federally sanctioned media channels. Sentenced to public execution, commuted to special service," Said Wilkins, as he stared at them all directly.

The room grew quiet, and the group of prisoners grew nervous.

"Your next question, of course, is 'why did our sentences get commuted? Why was it offered to us?' You all already know the answer to that. You had exemplary careers during your service with the Volunteer National Defense. In fact, all of you served in the same theater, though not in the same squads. When the U.K. collapsed at the start of the war, it was a shit show. We threw troops at it blindly hoping to take it back, and where most of them failed, you were all involved in the operation that succeeded in London," he said, pointing at each prisoner individually, "As such, I know that I can count on you to be creative and resilient. If you complete the mission, you'll go free."

"What's the catch?" Waters chimed in, knowing that the commander wasn't buttering them up for nothing.

"Your target is on this very island, it's-"

"That's why the gun mounts are facing inwards. You're keeping something from getting out, not the other way around," Feig said, in a very low, subdued voice.

"Correct. Again, a keen observation. One of the reasons you're here and not being executed on the Federal News Network tonight at 10," the commander said, making sure to squash any potential cockiness.

"What you're dealing with isn't like anything you've dealt with before. Your parents might have told you about monsters and ghouls when you were kids, but what we have here isn't a bedtime story to make you behave. This is tech we seized from the Chinese at the end of the war with a little bit of help from the Independent Republic of Hong Kong. We call it 'Manticore.' Some sort of bio-weapon. It's faster and stronger than anything we've seen, inside or outside of the war, and what it means for science will propel us into the future if we can study it."

"If it's so fast and strong, how did you even get it here?" Feig quipped.

"When we seized it from the Chinese, it was in containment. It was, inactive, for lack of a better word. By the time we transported it here, it was starting to wake up. It freed itself from its cage, and has been stuck here ever since," the Commander explained.

"So, you want us to track some fucking bio weapon - the four of us - that you can't do with a whole army? Why not send in the troops you already have? It sounds like a death sentence either way," Marquez said matter-of-factly.

"We've tried throwing regular troops at it, and they haven't stood a chance. This creature is smart - it knows the walls are manned and armed. It knows what the mounted guns can do. It eludes us when it wants to elude us, and it wipes out entire teams of men when it wants to kill. This creature thinks. It strategizes. It hunts."

"You're out of your god damned mind. There's no way that a four-man squad can take on a fucking monster. Are you guys hearing this? We're talking about a monster, for Christ's sake," Miller said anxiously.

"You can, and you will if you want to live. You were facing a death sentence either way. You were given an opportunity to commute that sentence. You took it. You can turn around right now, and you'll be executed the second you step foot outside the base, or perhaps you'll die fighting the Manticore, but one route gives you the option of freedom, the other does not."

"And you of the rulers and enforcers wonder why people like him and I try to tell people to fight back against you. We don't have any choice here, we only have the *illusion* of choice. You set this up so that we either do your dirty work for you and die, or we die anyway if we don't want to."

"Another keen observation, Mr. Waters. You're criminals against the state. You *should* be dead by all accounts, but here's your opportunity to gain freedom."

"Yeah? What kind of freedom? Getting rations of meat every week and trying desperately to feed ourselves with it, let alone a family? Getting told what job to do for the good of the country? Not being able to buy or sell anything that YOU haven't decided is permissable? I wouldn't fucking call that freedom. You can call yourselves the 'Democratic Republic' of the Americas, but that dog and pony show you put on every four years is a fucking joke."

"Without us you would be defenseless, so you can stow your anarchist rhetoric!"

"Without you we wouldn't have even gotten involved in the war! Without you we wouldn't have to struggle for scraps of food every god damned week. The whole world hates us because you couldn't mind your own fucking business!"

"ENOUGH!" the Commander finally snapped. "Either you are going to partake in this operation or you'll be executed outside."

The four unwilling soldiers looked around at each other with puzzled looks on their faces. Miller looked at Marquez - they knew they didn't have any other choice. Waters and Feig locked eyes.

"I don't want to die for them..." Feig said with a shred of fear in his voice.

"Neither do I..." Waters responded, clenching his fist slightly.

"Sleep on it, gentlemen. You'll be spending the night regardless. The guard outside will take you to the barracks. Get something to eat and get some rest, you'll need it."

The four slowly trickled out of the command center, and the guard led them along a swaying catwalk towards the sleeping quarters and mess hall.

***

The prisoners arrived at the mess hall - an unnervingly familiar place to them all. Eating sub-par food in exchange for putting their lives on the line for a politician they've never met, in a war zone they never agreed to go to, for a conflict they didn't start. Fodder for the war machine.

"Same shit food as I remember it. Cardboard and cat shit," Miller said.

"I'd say it's better than nothing, but I'm honestly not so sure," Marquez said, smirking.

"The coffee still sucks too," Waters joined in.

"That's because Colombia stopped farming it once the DRA took over. They shifted entirely to mineral fuels after the regime change," Feig added.

"Watch it, you'll get arrested for that kind of anti-government propaganda!" Marquez said with a laugh.

Feig and Waters hesitated for a moment, but ultimately burst out into laughter.

The four sat down in pairs across from each other - familiar mess hall fashion - and began eating the slop in front of them while commenting on its foul taste and texture. As they started to finish up, they began trading tales of their military experiences.

"So, you were there in London, right? Me and Miller here were in Knightsbridge, we had a squadron of thirty-six men. I was squad leader and he was my second in command. We were running diversion strategies and picking off sniper posts to help the main forces move forward into London proper."

"Yeah, we were in Stratford, a few clicks northeast of where you were. Feig here is the best damn mechanic on the whole planet Earth - and not just cars and trucks, this guy knows his way around machines, weapons, artillery, you name it", Waters said. Feig blushed.

"What he's getting at is that I'm a bit of a... a nerd. I always had a knack for engineering. I was actually training at a shop in south Jersey before the DRA swooped in and told me I was getting deployed," Feig said shyly.

"Whoa, so that means you're the one who commandeered the enemy artillery in Stratford? Holy shit!" Marquez said shocked.

"That's right, you could almost say this guy single handedly turned the tide for that whole theater, because the main forces trying to come into West End and Shepherd's Bush were getting fuckin' battered with shells. Still..." Waters trailed off.

"And you're a Jersey boy! I'm from Camden, born and raised. Miller's one of those degenerates from north Jersey" Marquez interjected.

"Hey, hey, asshole, I'm from the southern tip of Monmouth county, that's *central* Jersey, alright?" Miller defended himself.

"There's no such thing as 'central' Jersey, man. You might as well be a New Yorker!" Marquez jested with air quotes.

"Ahh screw you. How about you Waters?" Miller deflected.

"South Philly for about fifteen years, then moved to Delco. Lived in Norwood for a while, but moved a whole five minutes to Collingdale," Waters said.

"Shit, a couple of Philly boys and a New Yorker!" Marquez said with a snigger. "Small world man, and here we are at the gates of hell again."

"Yeah... it's hard to count the Stratford mission as a win when you really look at it... The amount of people we killed, and for what?" Feig said with a pained look on his face.

"That was also when we realized that the governments that had us killing each other didn't give a single shit about us. The so-called enemies' government didn't give a shit about their people - we were all just bodies for the political machine. No one ever thinks about that. They drill it into us in school to obey and worship authority. They drill it into us at boot camp that we're expendable, and they have the balls to tell us it's a fuckin' honorable death. Ha!" Waters said incensed. "The worst part is, for a short while I fuckin' bought it. The reality is, a bunch of limp dick politicians sitting in their cozy offices call the shots while we get sent to march to an early grave. We were lucky enough to make it out... and that's when we knew we had to tell the people back home... they don't need a government to tell them how to live. They don't need politicians dragging them into wars with countries we have no business being in. They don't need their paychecks stolen from them to fund their meddling bullshit."

"By the sound of it, though, you guys were ready to take the bullet option up in the CC. Can't spread your message if you're dead," Miller said with a slight chuckle.

"You're right, and it's something I've been thinking about ever since we left. I'd hate to die doing anything at the request of our oppressors... but I'd also hate to die knowing that I could have done more to free our people - and I'm not just talking about what used to be North America, I'm talking about the whole DRA. Every single person should be able to live how they want without some wolf in sheep's clothing dictating where and how they should live, what they can eat, what they can smoke. Ugh!" Waters said with rage in his voice.

"So you're in then?" Marquez said inquisitively.

"I guess so. One last mission for the state against our will? Sounds fitting."

Feig smirked. Marquez looked over at Miller who seemed captivated by Waters' words. He looked down at his empty plate of battle rations and began to question himself - what authority do they truly have outside of the fact that they're the ones with the guns and they make the rules? Marquez now understood Waters' and Feig's apprehension at blindly agreeing to assist Commander Wilkins, but he also understood why they don't have a choice.

"I'm gonna get some sleep. It's been years since I've had a proper brief, and quite frankly I'm not looking forward to it," Waters said as he stood up. Feig shortly followed and they both went off to their bunks. Marquez and Miller sat silently at the table, taking in the conversation they just had, each independently analyzing the situation they find themselves in.

"Hey, Joey?"

"Yeah?" Marquez said, coming out of a thousand-yard stare.

"What do you think about all that stuff they were saying? I mean, there's always been someone in charge, you know? Calling the shots... do you really think the world would operate without it?"

"Honestly, at first, I thought they were talking out their asses... but truthfully, what do they REALLY do? Road maintenance? You know the roads in Jersey - they're a fucking nightmare... After the war, they took over everything and people are starving to death. People are getting executed, shit, WE would have been executed... I don't know man..." Marquez paused for a long time. "But I'd like to see it happen. Anything has to be better than the way we're living now. C'mon, enough heady shit for one night, we better get some sleep," Marquez and Miller headed off to the sleeping quarters.

Marquez laid in his cot, staring at the cot above his. He fought hard to forget the war. He tried so many times to convince himself that he was just following orders, but now he was having second thoughts. Could he have done more? Could he have said no? After tossing and turning, he finally fell asleep.

***

"Miller! Move back, gather the rest of the squad and wait for my order!" Marquez screamed as the shells burst around them. He sprinted up to a barricade next to a Harvey Nichols outlet store. The civilians were running through the streets and alleyways to avoid the artillery fire. Others were dead in the street, missing limbs, and screaming in agony as their final breath. He heard a piercing scream from his left and he looks over, into a dark alley way, lit only by the dim fires on the surrounding buildings. A group of men had a young woman, who couldn't have been any older than twenty, pinned down, as they tore at her clothes like wild animals.

He cleared the chamber of his rifle, loaded a new magazine and racked a round. He aimed carefully to make sure he didn't hit the girl. He fired three spaced shots and took out three of them. Two remained. One of them was struggling to get his pants back up, Marquez took aim once more, using the heads-up display in his helmet to target the man's neck. The bullet ripped through his throat and he collapsed with his pants around his ankles. The other man struggled to ready his sidearm, and Marquez took the shot. The man collapsed to the ground. His pistol clanked three times before it finally rested a few feet away from the girl.

"It's okay, I'm not going to hurt you. I want to get you out of here."

The girl was a local. She quivered with fear, the tears were still wet on her cheeks.

"It's okay, I promise, please we have to get you out of here." he insisted.

Her right hand slowly moved towards the pistol.

"Don't! Don't do that! Please... just come with me, we're going to get you out of here."

Her arm was visibly shaking, and her eyes were completely locked with his.

She grabbed the pistol clumsily and pointed it at him.

"FUCK!" he screamed.

Two shots were fired. He looked at the wall to his left and saw the hole where her bullet landed.

She fell to her knees, as if in slow motion, while the life left her body through the hole in her chest.

Marquez began to cry as he heard his communications channel open.

"Marquez?! Where are you? I've got the squad rounded up at block B, what is your order?" Miller hollered on the radio.

He woke up from his sleep and wiped his brow, letting out a deep sigh.

"Can't sleep?" Miller whispered.

"Yeah..."

"The girl?"

Marquez was silent.

"Look, man, I know it's fucked up, but some day you're going to have to forgive yourself," Miller said, peeking down from his bunk.

"Just go back to sleep," Marquez said in a defeated whisper.

The two faded back into sleep for what seemed like a few minutes when they were abruptly woken up by Commander Wilkins on the loudspeaker.

"Rise and shine, gentlemen. Grab a quick bite to eat and then come see me in my office."

The four hurriedly scarfed some of the cardboard and cat shit breakfast provisions from the mess hall and got suited up in their bunks. A guard was waiting for them at the door to take them up to the command center. They trotted up the stairs behind the guard and approached the glass encased office. They piled in through the door and lined up in front of the large desk.

"Good morning" the commander said exhaling a large plume of cigar smoke, "I hope you're all well fed and well rested. Have you come to a decision?"

"Yes. We'll do it," Marquez said assuredly.

"Does he speak for all of you?" Wilkins said, gesturing at the other three prisoners.

"We've all agreed to do it," Said Waters, holding back a bit of anger.

"Good. Last night you got a quick overview of what you're dealing with, but today you'll be getting everything we know. Habits, patterns, battle specs - to the best of our ability, and so on and so forth. Mr. Schuck will take you to the war room to go over everything with you. Excuse me one moment." The commander leaned over to his lapel and began broadcasting over the loudspeaker, "Mr. Schuck, please report to the command center and escort our visitors to strategic ops."

The four prisoners waited anxiously for the mysterious Mr. Schuck to arrive. The commander sighed another plume of smoke into the room and turned his head down to the screen on his desk. Seemingly lost in maps, graphs, and metrics. The subtle beeping of electronics permeated the room, tearing through the dreadful silence that followed the end of the radio broadcast. It was then that Marquez noticed something that rattled him to his core. He heard no birds or insects from the otherwise lush woods on the island. Not a single feather beating in the wind, not a single chirp or tweet. Whatever was in those woods had either scared off the wildlife or consumed it.

Mr. Schuck entered the room without anyone noticing.

"If you'll follow me please."

The group jumped and turned around in shock.

"Jesus Christ, man, I nearly ruined this fresh gear!" Waters laughed.

The commander chuckled, "He tends to do that, you'll have to forgive him. You get used to it after a while."

Marquez noticed the beginning of a smile at the corner of the mysterious man's stern lips. Their eyes met, and the man abruptly turned around and began walking out of the office and onto the shaky catwalk. The prisoners hesitantly followed.

After many minutes of walking along the catwalk gazing down at the eerily silent woods, they arrived upon another installation built into the wall surrounding the island, straddled by two mounted turrets pointed in towards the island. A large cement structure, similar to the command center but with significantly less glass. The imposing edifice was constructed with stylistic sharp angles and slopes into the structure. The inactive spotlights were comforting to the group, simply knowing that it wasn't going to be dark for some time. The security door hissed open as the hydraulic locks disengaged. Mr. Schuck gestured to the group to sit down at the chairs around the war table, as they called it, in the center of the room. The rounded rectangular table had a tetrahedron jutting out of the center, which projected a three-dimensional topographical map of the island. Countless monitors draped the walls, each with their own complex visualizations of various bits of data that the group couldn't decipher. They looked around in awe, as they had never seen anything like this, not even during the war.

"Welcome to Strategic Operations. My name is Christopher Schuck, I'm the head of this division on Petty Island."

"Not to sound like an asshole, but what exactly are you head of? Outside of a few guards, you, and the commander, we haven't seen a single soul on this island," Waters remarked.

"Valid question, though the answer should be obvious. The Petty Island operation is primarily subterranean."

"Makes sense, that way it wouldn't be visible via satellite or spy drones. The most they'd get is an otherwise nondescript island on the Delaware," Feig said, sounding oddly impressed with their surreptitiousness. "I guess you'll go to any lengths to keep things hidden from the public, right?"

"It's for their protection, Mr. Feig. Surely, you've heard the old adage 'what they don't know won't hurt them', correct?" Schuck responded curtly. "Your extremism aside, even a man like yourself - and Mr. Waters - can understand the need for secrecy every now and then, right? Considering your lack of it was how we found you in the first place."

Feig put on a grimace and looked down at the table.

"Now, to the matters at hand. Commander Wilkins gave you a brief overview of what you'll be dealing with. The Manticore. What he didn't tell you, I'll be taking the opportunity to divulge."

Marquez and Miller looked at each other with looks of mixed anxiety and fear.

"What you're looking at here is a topographical map of the island. Ground and water level. The Manticore doesn't come out during the day. We've swept the entire island without losing a single man, but without a single trace of it either. You will be using this knowledge to your advantage to learn your way around without fear of conflict, and of course with the safety of the turrets surrounding the installation. Now-"

Schuck gestured his hands above a small, spherical, interactive console. The map faded into the center of the tetrahedron on the table, which hummed, whirred, and emitted a bright glow. The picture it projected horrified the prisoners, who sat speechless in their chairs.

"This is the Manticore. What you're seeing is the result of Chinese organic weapon development. We seized it at the end of the war, as it must have been in its preliminary stages. By the time we had it brought here, it was becoming fully formed. It single-handedly wiped out a squad of twelve men, and it has been secluded here ever since."

"What the fuck...?" Marquez said, quivering under his breath.

"From what we were able to gather from preliminary scans, we have only a rudimentary understanding of its physiology. Its exterior is made up of a thick carapace covering hardened flesh. The carapace is similar to psoriasis - it uses purposeful cell

26

duplication at an alarming rate to create 'plaques' that form a natural protective barrier. From that, I'm sure you can infer that it has enhanced regenerative abilities, but it's not instantaneous. We've wounded the creature countless times, but it retreats for sometimes days at a time. On our next encounters, it's back to one hundred percent combat capability, based on combat metrics gained from the troops we've pitched against it. The tail possesses a biological toxin that we haven't seen before, but it's similar in behavior to that of the blue ring octopus off the coasts of Australia. Initially, minor pain, followed by numbness and excessive bleeding at the site of the sting. Within ten minutes, the numbness will spread, followed by nausea, blurry vision, and paralysis beginning at the extremities and working its way inward. Eventually, full paralysis, requiring mechanical ventilation. None of the men who have been subjected to the toxin have survived."

"So, if your troops can't handle this thing in groups of twelve, and it can run away and regenerate whenever it pleases, what makes you think we're going to fare any better?" Marquez said, striking the table with his hand.

"First, all of you were instrumental in the success of your respective operations in the London theater. Secondly, we'll be arming you with experimental ballistics technology that our team has been working on here to take down the Manticore. You all have exemplary skill in tactics, you all tested in the top first percentile for weapons training, and most importantly, you all want to go free."

"Is this some kind of glorified weapon R&D bullshit?" Waters exclaimed.

"Despite what you and your extremist friend may think, no, this is not 'some glorified R&D bullshit.' The weapons and ammunition we're arming you with have been specifically designed for this target and this target alone."

"Yeah, and I'm sure you'll just happen to find another purpose for them in your research. We're fuckin' guinea pigs."

"Think what you will, Mr. Waters, but the bottom line is that you will have the equipment you need to succeed. It's up to you to make it happen. I've already notified the armory, you'll have full access to our stock, and you've been cleared for the experimental tech. You've still got six hours of safe daylight. Go get equipped, and when you're ready, head back towards the command center, take the stairs down from where you first came in. The guard there will open the gate. Any of the information we went over and more detailed specs can be accessed on the HUDs within your helmets."

The prisoners stood up and left Strategic Operations, meandering along the catwalk.

"Any of you guys notice there's no animals here? No birds, no bugs - nothin'," Marquez said, waiting to be out of earshot of Schuck.

"I knew something was off. I mean, everything about this is off, but something didn't feel right" Miller responded.

"You mean like having to kill a fuckin' monster? Some twisted creation funded by people that had no idea they were paying for it, with a government bureaucrat playing with himself for the fat raise he's going to get at their expense? Yeah, something's off alright," Waters grunted scathingly.

"I don't even know why they think we'll be any good here in the woods. The only combat we saw was in the metro," Miller said.

"They call cities concrete jungles for a reason. Buildings are the trees. Trash cans and parked cars are the bushes. Every living being in it is a wild animal. Strategically, the same principles apply," Feig said timidly.

"Between Philly and Jersey, shit might as well have been the jungle," Marquez added.

The conversation ended abruptly, as the gravity of their situation set in. As they marched towards the armory, they each thought about their lives before the war. They thought about their lives before the DRA. Marquez thought about his car. He put so much work into it, only to have it impounded and scrapped for the war effort. Miller thought about his girlfriend, Stacie, who died during the siege on the beaches of Portrush, Northern Ireland. Feig thought back to his shop in Haddon Heights. Fixing engines, helping out his neighbors. Waters didn't have a great memory to think back on. His wife had just recently passed away suddenly from misdiagnosed heart disease. Philadelphia Federal Hospital had denied him and his family any compensation. The business they ran together suffered without her. The back taxes ended up piling up until he had to file for bankruptcy. He lost his home, his business, his dignity, but most of all his family. He would have traded it all to have them back.

They arrived at the armory.

***

"Those who are capable of tyranny are capable of perjury to sustain it"

— Lysander Spooner

Chapter 2 - Invaders

As the prisoners stepped inside the armory, the backlights kicked on, like the liquor rack at a bar, illuminating the weapons scattered about the walls. Pistols, rifles, explosives, ammunition, protective gear, and everything in between. The armory clerk didn't look up from his info screen, lazily reading the news. Marquez and Miller headed for the defensive gear - protective layers of anti-puncture mesh, adrenal stimulants, and stun grenades. Waters beelined for the rifles, spotting a vintage AR configuration. Feig, unsurprisingly to the rest of the group, started inspecting the various tech and gadgets on the far side of the wall - grappling hooks, nets, portable barriers, and all of the things that would interest a tinkerer like him.

"You won't be needing any of that stuff for daytime. Just grab a couple of rifles and head to the gate," Said the clerk, as he sat still without picking his head up from his info screen.

"If you say so," Marquez said sarcastically. The group grabbed some standard issue rifles usually reserved for kids entering their first year of mandatory service, or for field exercises. Marquez had the feeling this didn't quite qualify as a standard field exercise but didn't feel like arguing the point with someone who couldn't bother to make eye contact with the people he was speaking to. *He must be from New York*, he thought and grinned.

They proceeded out of the armory and checked in with the guard at the main gate on ground level.

Before anyone had a chance to speak, the guard, seemingly not wanting to sit around with small talk, cut right to the chase. "Schuck called ahead and cleared you guys. Make sure you're back by 1900, you don't want to be out there when it gets dark, and we're on lockdown at 1900 on the dot. Gate won't open at that point, and you're on your own. You'll receive warning notifications in your helmets at one hour, thirty minutes, and ten minutes until lockdown."

No one said anything in response, they got the message loud and clear. The klaxon blared as the massive gate depressurized and began to slide open. Marquez noticed a slight smirk, almost scoffing, on the guard's face. *He's probably seen people like us go through this gate and never come back. He's laughing at us,* he thought to himself. They trudged across the cold, metallic threshold and crunched the leaves beneath their boots. The klaxon blared once again, and they turned around to see a smiling guard and the gate to safety closing behind them.

Marquez started off in a random direction, staying relatively close to the walls.

"Good idea, we'll get a feel for the perimeter first and work our way in," Waters said, breaking the silence of the woods.

"That's the plan. I want to make sure we're comfortable getting to the wall and the turrets first and foremost. They said this thing is smart enough to stay away from them, so we can use that to our advantage," Marquez replied coldly.

They continued deeper in, making sure to keep the perimeter walls within their vision. The silence of the island was starting to affect them. Feig began to fidget. Waters began tapping on his thigh pads. Marquez became hyper focused, trying to shrug the unnatural feeling of a completely silent woodland. Miller tripped.

"Shit!" he exclaimed.

Waters began to laugh, while Marquez checked on his friend. "You okay brother?" He extended his hand to Miller, helping him back on his feet.

"Something must have jumped out in front of me, god damn."

Feig was the first to notice the handle sticking out of the ground - the one that jumped in front of Miller.

Marquez opened comms and said "Schuck, we've got a hatch out here, was that map you showed us incomplete?"

"No. As I said, you can see more details on what I showed you inside your helmet. That hatch leads to the old installation, it's logically the only place where the Manticore could hide during the day. That said, we've annexed off the old installation from the new," Schuck said in between the static.

"So basically, it's a death trap," Marquez quipped.

"Precisely."

"Are there other entrance and exit points?"

"Yes, they're scattered around the island. Some, like the one mister Miller tripped over, are maintenance hatches that lead to the spaces in between the main halls and offices for network and utility repairs. You will also come across some small enclosures, these lead to the aforementioned main halls. We cut power to the annex, so vision will be limited even with headlamps."

"Copy that. We'll stay above ground and keep at it, but we're going to look at any schematics you have for the annex when we get back. 1900 correct?"

"Yes, mister Marquez. I'll prepare the schematics for viewing when you get back."

"Thanks, Chuck" Marquez said with a snigger.

"It's 'Schuck', mister Marquez"

"What's that, Buck? I think we're getting some interference," Waters joined in.

"There's no interference - this island isn't that big, gentlemen" Schuck was not amused.

"Sorry, Mack, can't hear you," Miller said, Marquez closed comms shortly after.

The group laughed at Schuck's expense for a few minutes. It was a welcome distraction to the thought that the Manticore could be following and listening to their every move and word. A reality they would soon have to confront.

They continued through the island, following the wall and noting anything important on their HUD maps. Marquez pulled up an overlay of all annex entry points and highlighted them on his interface. The helmet interface could be clunky and clustered at times, but from what he could tell, there were at least twelve maintenance hatches and six main entrance points. *At least if these are connected,* he thought, *we might be able to go in, look around, and bee line towards another exit to drop in and out. Far less risky than going in blind and getting trapped in a corner.*

Feig stopped walking with a concerned and fearful look on his face. The rest of the group kept walking until Waters finally noticed.

"You alright?"

"Shhhh," Feig said, putting the index finger of his right hand up into the air. He turned on group comms to be able to speak quietly directly into the group's helmets. "Come here. Listen."

The group gently treaded back to Feig and formed a small circle.

"What is it?" Waters inquired.

"Wait for it!" Feig said, uncharacteristically with authority.

They waited patiently, each hearing the air leaving their own noses. They breathed heavier and faster, their heart rates increased as the anxiety built, and then they heard it. A dull, metallic clank, so faint it was almost inaudible.

"Big deal, Feig. Schuck said there are maintenance tunnels and shit underneath of us. Could be an old pipe" Waters said dismissively.

What sounded like a faint, agonized moan filled their ears a moment later. A shiver ran down Marquez's spine, and Miller got goosebumps. It was following them, and it didn't sound enthused.

Marquez opened comms, "Schuck, I think it's following us, we just heard it underground."

"Sorry, mister Marquez, I believe I'm getting a bit of interference," Schuck said, shortly before closing the comms channel.

"Alright, we kind of had that coming," Miller said.

They looked at each other for a brief second, looked down at the sub-par weaponry in their hands, and they remembered that this was for scouting only. Feig looked up at the sun and saw it was beginning to set.

"One hour until lockdown" a disembodied voice announced in their helmets.

"Marquez, how far away are we from the main gate?"

"Looks like we're just about two thirds of the way around. Let's pick up the pace and finish this loop, we'll end up back at the gate."

They began to jog along the wall, muscle memory kicking in from the war. Their adrenaline began to flow, but that adrenaline was laced with regret and fear. Regret for the countless innocent lives they took and had taken from them. The regret that they followed orders when they had no desire to kill. The regret that they would have to do it again. The fear, however, came from the dull metallic clanking getting louder through the ground, and keeping pace with them.

"It's fucking following us, man!" Waters said between breaths.

"We're still along the walls, it's not going to come out and get lit up by the turrets," Marquez responded.

"Well, it sure sounds like it's thinking about it"

The jog turned into a sprint, and they could see the main gate around the bend. The subterranean thumps and clangs seemed to slow and die down. The Manticore knew where it was relative to the surface. *How long has this thing been here?* Marquez thought.

Walters opened comms to Schuck. "Schuck get your man to open the gate, we're coming in hot!"

He heard no response, the comms channel closed. They ran faster as the creature slowed down and hesitated. As they approached, they heard the klaxon blaring as the gate opened. They ran through and came to a stop. Marquez leaned up against the wall to catch his breath, while Miller laid on the ground, staring up at the canopy of leaves above the installation. Waters popped his visor up and pulled out a mangled cigarette. He pulled a butane lighter from the front pocket of his suit with a trembling hand and lit it, taking a long drag. He exhaled a plume of smoke and breathed heavily, catching his breath while simultaneously throwing it away to breathe the fire from his lungs. Feig sat down, exhausted, when suddenly they all heard a disembodied woman in their helmets.

"Ten minutes to lockdown."

"How the hell did we miss the thirty-minute warning?" Miller said, sitting up from laying on the ground.

"Couldn't hear it over the sound of shitting our pants, I guess" Waters laughed.

"How are you laughing right now? Have you already forgotten that we're here against our will?

And for what? To stave off an execution? Never mind the fact that we just ran from a fucking government bio weapon that's living underground!" Feig exclaimed.

They were taken aback, and silent. They knew Feig was right. The gravity of the situation they were in shouldn't have been lost on them so soon, but they were taught to brush off tragedy and injustice for the sake of making them better soldiers. The training they received, from compulsory school all the way to mandatory military service, was all to make sure that they would follow orders no matter what. They pulled the triggers on the weapons of politicians.

"Y-you're right, Feig. I know this whole situation is fucked... but like you said, we're here against our will, man. We're not going anywhere anytime soon, except in a body bag. I don't like it any more than you do, but we have to work with the very institution we're actively trying to dismantle. Irony is a cruel bastard, and it's not lost on me, but if taking down that fuckin' thing means we can help save people from the same fate, or worse yet the public execution we were supposed to get, then fuck it. We'll lick the boots one more time so that hopefully no one else ever has to, ever again."

Marquez and Miller took in Waters' words carefully. Life in the DRA was worse than they thought. It was bad enough their whole lives were run for them by someone else, but the stark realization that they were basically livestock, mindless drones, bred to be loyal servants, penetrated them to their cores.

"Let's get over to strategic ops and see what Schuck has for us. If this thing is using the tunnels of the annex, we need to know what its escape routes are. If we're ever going to fight for freedom - actual freedom - ever again, we need to make it off of this island," Marquez said after a long silence punctuated Waters' speech.

Everyone stood up and gathered themselves and silently headed up the stairs to the catwalk to head to strategic operations.

***

As they arrived to strategic operations, the sun was almost fully set, with the creamsicle colored sky just barely lighting the way. Strangely, the guard that was supposed to be there was gone, and the door was already open.

"Gentlemen, have a seat. I've prepared the schematics of the annex for you to look over," Schuck said without acknowledging anything the group experienced.

"So, we're not going to talk about this 'Manticore' of yours chasing us underground?" Waters said angrily.

"To do so would be to waste time, we would only cover what we already know. Sit, and I can show you the annex so you know what you're getting into tomorrow."

"What's tomorrow?"

"Your expedition during the day drew more attention from the Manticore than we've gotten in months, and we don't know why that is. Considering that you were patrolling the outside of the island - rather prudently, I might add - and it followed you, that leads me to believe that it's predominantly spending its time in the maintenance tunnels. You'll be entering the main halls, and you'll be aware of all entry and exit points, both from maintenance into the main area, and from both areas back to the surface. You'll be going during the daytime so you can escape to daylight if necessary."

"You mean when necessary," Marquez added.

"The Manticore has been mostly dormant outside of night sorties, and during the daytime we hadn't heard a peep or even registered any movement until the four of you went out there. Now, onto the important things."

The group sat down at their seats, Waters crossed his arms defiantly while Feig sat and looked down at the table averting his eyes. Marquez and Miller plopped their helmets on the table and looked at Schuck with a sarcastic expectance. Schuck once again waved his hand above the interface, and a large multi-layered three-dimensional map of the annex filled the room from the tetrahedron.

"Here is the maintenance hatch mister Miller discovered on your exploratory mission this afternoon. Here are the other eleven. Many are on the outer perimeter, but there are four that directly connect to the main areas of operations, and as such are viable escape routes between the two."

The red indicators each appeared on screen with a distinctive beeping sound. All relevant information to them appeared alongside each - distance from the main gate, distance from each other, nearest exit point, spatial dimensions, and more.

"Here are the six main entryways to the offices and operations areas. You'll notice that they appear to be nondescript storage sheds, and that's because they are. Inside are elevators shafts that offer you a way in and out as well. The elevators are currently unpowered, but we'll divert power from the main grid to the annex systems to allow them to be used. The elevators have hydraulic security doors that are rated for high grade demolitions and ballistics. If you encounter the Manticore and cannot maintain your current position, fall back to an elevator if need be."

"We're going in there tomorrow?!" Miller said with trepidation.

"What did you expect, mister Miller? You're already trained. You already have the skills above and beyond our regular soldiers, much to my chagrin, and now you're getting the information you need to be able to deal with the problem. Were you expecting an extended vacation?"

"Not a vacation, but at least a few more fucking days of preparation! We might as well be going in blind!"

"You forget, mister Miller, that we're going to be arming you with state of the art weaponry and ammunition that has been catered specifically to deal with this threat, and while we haven't had a chance to properly test it as our own men get slaughtered, you four will do better than our own men, because you want to live, and you want to be free, but that's enough waxing poetic. Let's continue."

Schuck switched the display back to that of the Manticore, and each element of the Manticore's body had information gathered and displayed next to it.

"As you can see here, we've tried traditional ballistics, even armor piercing rounds and explosives, and while they seem to wound the Manticore, it does nothing more than slow it down. We've created ammunition that also delivers a neurotoxin that we're hoping can do more than slow it, if we can-"

"You're hoping? So, you haven't even tried these new weapons out, and we get to be the guinea pigs?" Marquez interjected.

"I can assure you, we've spent more than enough resources developing this technology. There are always unknowns and externalities, but logic dictates that they will be drastically more effective than traditional ballistics."

"So THAT'S what the eighty percent tax rate was for, eh Chuck?" Waters said with a smirk.

"If you want to continue your childish game with my name, feel free to do so tomorrow in the annex."

Waters grunted, rolled his eyes, and looked away.

Schuck once again waved his hand and the display changed to a chemical structure.

"Now, the neurotoxin imparts a sort of... hyperactive amyotrophic lateral sclerosis. The Manticore's regenerative abilities are most likely controlled in some part by neurons in the brain, but instead of acting on the voluntary muscles, it acts on cells' reproductive abilities as a whole. We don't expect it will stop it completely, but it should dampen it enough to keep it down and non-lethal long enough to find a more permanent solution. Since the neurotoxin has been accelerated, it won't last an extremely long amount of time. A few hours, at least, in order to contain it. The rate at which the Manticore would metabolize such a thing is an unknown, but based on extrapolated data gathered on its rate of regeneration, it should be long enough."

"I'm hearing lots of 'should', 'may, and 'possibly' in there. Sounds like a lot more unknowns than you're making it seem like" Marquez said.

"All we need you to do is subdue the Manticore. We'll send in a containment team to handle the rest."

"So, we just go in, shoot this thing with a neurotoxin, HOPE that it works, and if it does, we radio you to send in the containment team?"

"Precisely."

"By the sound of it, you're more than just a strategist. Are you also one of the lab rats that came up with this poison bullet?" Waters said.

"Very astute. Commander Wilkins was smart in choosing you for this operation. Your observation skills are far above what I'd expect based on every other interaction we've had, but yes, I also run the science department, which is the primary function of this island. Getting back yet again to the topic at hand," Schuck said, with the slightest hint of anger in his voice. The group derailing his briefing was clearly getting to him. He wasn't used to dealing with such vocal parties. "I suppose you should have enough information by now to handle tomorrow's sortie. Remember, you have the elevators to fall back to, and-"

"And it doesn't come out during the daytime, so if we have to abort, we can come up to the surface. Got it," Marquez interrupted.

"Correct. I've sent orders to the armory to give you the weapons and ammunition as I mentioned earlier. The weapons feel and behave identically to what you're used to, but we've altered the amount of combustion that happens in the chamber so as not to diminish the efficacy neurotoxin."

"Is that going to have any effect on reliable range? Or drop?" Waters questioned.

"Nothing noticeable. You will suffer a small decrease in propulsion, but for something that usually fires at over two thousand feet per second, a few hundred feet per second shouldn't affect your combat ability. I recommend you all go get something to eat and rest up. When you wake up, suit up and head directly to the armory. Once you've secured your weaponry, head to the main gate. I'll give you one final briefing before you head out."

"Copy that, Chuck," Waters said, hoping to see another rise out of Schuck.

"Dismissed, gentlemen."

***

The group plodded out of strategic operations and began their trek back across the catwalk to head towards the mess hall. The first breeze for what felt like an eternity came through the trees as the sun began to completely vanish along the horizon. No one said a word, not even Waters who loathed an awkward silence spoke up. They each knew that tomorrow was going to be pivotal in either their freedom or their death.

As they arrived at the stairs to the mess hall, the silence finally broke. A low rumble and what seemed to be a groan, reminiscent of what they heard while out on patrol earlier in the afternoon.

"Hard to have an appetite knowing what we're going up against," Marquez said, "I know we need to eat, but fuck is it going to be hard to get down with that... thing out there just waiting for us."

"I'm trying not to think about it until we're in it. Save the adrenaline n' all," Miller responded. "Let's get some slop and some rest, and we can focus on shitting ourselves to death tomorrow," Waters chuckled, and Feig cracked a rare smile, if only for a second. The four entered the mess hall, shocked to see a spread of delicious steaks, roasted vegetables, and a bottle of unlabeled wine.

"Good evening gentlemen. Since tomorrow is your first real sortie, I had the provisions officer get some real food for you," Wilkins' voice crackled over the speakers.

"Is this our last meal?" Waters said, laughing.

"Given your skills, I would hope not, but if it is, I hope it's sufficient for you."

"New York strip, some demi-glace, haricot verts and garlic smashed potatoes? Hmph, I guess it'll do."

"Where in the sweet fuck did you hear about demi-glace or haricot verts, Waters?" said a gobsmacked Marquez.

"What do you think I used to do before the shit hit the fan?"

"You were a chef?!"

"Yeah. Me and..."

"Let's just drop it guys-" Feig interjected, but was cut off.

"It's fine, Feig. Me and my wife had a restaurant in Collingswood. We couldn't afford a spot in Philly, so we just hopped over the bridge to your guys' neck of the woods. You might have even eaten there."

"Collingswood? On Haddon Ave? You had a restaurant on restaurant row? I used to take my girlfriends there to eat all the time! You could get anything there - Japanese, Thai, fusion, Mexican. What was your restaurant called?"

"Doesn't really matter now... Right before the war started, my wife got really sick. Cervical cancer. Since we owned our own business, and it was in Jersey, we got taxed out the ass. Small business tax was almost twenty thousand alone. We made too much to qualify for the awful 'free' federal insurance, but not enough to get private insurance and pay our bills and workers. I took her to get treated anyway." His eyes began to shimmer and well up in such a way that was barely perceptible. "I had to watch her wither for two weeks, and like the flick of a light switch, she was taken from me. I had to close the business, I owed twenty thousand and change in back taxes, and then another sixty thousand for her treatments out of pocket. My kids got taken away because the government decided I was 'unfit' to watch my own kids, despite the fact that I was liquidating everything in the restaurant and still putting food on the table. I signed up to join the military a week before the conscription started, because I was looking for a way to die... Then I met Feig at basic, who reminded me that the world isn't completely full of scumbags and murderers. He was a mess!" Waters laughed, with tears in his eyes. "Kept dropping shit, tripping over shit. I'm honestly surprised it was you that tripped over that hatch, Miller, I'm sure destiny had Feig lined right up for it!"

Everyone burst out into laughter, even Feig.

"I'm really sorry to hear that, man... We all lost someone, or something, when we had to go fight..." Marquez said looking down at his plate of food. "I had no idea you had it so bad..."

"That's just it. I didn't have it so bad when she was here. We struggled, but we were happy. When the government made it mandatory to have insurance and we didn't qualify for their free insurance program, it was actually cheaper to pay the yearly fine and just go to the urgent care clinics. These cock suckers have the nerve to call me an extremist for believing that people don't need them to live their lives, yet it was their direct interference that made it so private insurance skyrocketed in price, and who knows, maybe she'd still be here. Maybe I could have had more time with her... I'm not the only one that has lost loved ones because of this exact bullshit, which is why I got so fervent about spreading the message of freedom - TRUE fuckin' freedom. It's also the reason I got arrested and brought here to have this very conversation. Ain't that a bitch?"

Marquez and Miller nodded.

"You're a pretty, uh, extroverted guy, to say the least. I'm curious how you and Feig ended up getting along in any kind of way, no offense Feig, you're just much more quiet," Marquez said, attempting to lift the somber tone of the conversation.

"It's funny actually. While he was fumbling around basic, I was getting into trouble. I sought out the first person I could to get me anything I could use to ease the pain. Coke, booze, ADHD meds, you name it. Anything that could be out of my system by the next drug test, I had it. One night I was feeling especially sorry for myself and went a little hard. I was in my late twenties then, and the hangovers were exponential, but this wasn't a hangover. I almost died."

"Holy shit, man..." Miller said, surprised.

"Yeah... Feig found me down for the count. He tracked down my dealer, got me Benzos and a respirator and got my heart rate stable. Didn't tell anybody, because as you know, they executed anyone for drug offenses on base. He saved my life twice, and you know what the first thing he fuckin' says to me?"

Miller and Marquez looked at each other with inquisitive smiles.

"Try the Benzos by themselves first next time, asshole."

Miller and Marquez burst out laughing, Feig had an uncharacteristically large smile, like he was holding back the desire to laugh.

"I'm lying there with a respirator on my face hoping my heart doesn't stop, and he's busting my fucking balls for doing too many uppers! After that, we looked out for each other on base. When we got deployed, we looked out for each other on the battlefield. He showed me a lot about engineering and how to fix things. Comes in handy when eighty percent of your money is funding the war effort and the federal insurance you don't qualify for. He, surprisingly enough, couldn't make macaroni and cheese if his life depended on it, so I showed him how to cook. The rest, as painfully cliché as it is to say, is history."

"Jesus Christ, man. I partied hard back in the day, but it sounds like you were trying to die," Miller said with a small chuckle.

"Honestly, I was. I lost everything. I signed up because, really, it was the only thing to keep me busy. My wife was gone, my business closed, I was never going to see my kids again... I was honestly hoping for death. When he saved me though, I realized that there are still people to care about. There are still causes to get behind. People can help each other if they want to. They don't need the government to put a gun to their head to do it. People can also choose not to help people if they don't want to. That's the beauty of true freedom, and that's what I fight for now. That and this asshole right here," he said, gesturing to Feig.

"How am I supposed to follow that?" Marquez said, throwing his hands in the air.

"It's not a competition, or anything. I don't know... it felt good getting some of that off my chest. If this thing kills us, I wouldn't have anyone else to tell anyway. If any of you make it, you can keep it alive, you know?"

There was a short silence. Miller, Marquez, and even Feig who already knew the story, took a moment to digest what they heard.

"Enough with the heavy though, let's not let these steaks go to waste - look, even the fat is rendered properly. They must have gotten an actual chef on deck. Must have put a gun to his head and told him to make them perfect, because they sure as hell weren't paying him anything!"

The group returned to a familiar laughter. Waters didn't want to bring everyone down, but he wanted to make sure his story was told. They enjoyed the beautiful sear on the steaks, seasoned with salt and pepper, perfumed with fresh rosemary and garlic. Cooked to a perfect medium rare, tender and juicy. The salty, garlicky butter with chopped bits of parsley coated the potatoes, offering them a taste and texture that none of them had tasted in years. When the DRA put regulations on protein and fat sales, the best the average person could do was margarine and, if they were very lucky, a few ounces of flank steak a week. The haricot verts were blanched and tossed in warm butter with minced shallot, offering a vibrant green color and a beautiful al dente snap as they bit into them. They savored each bite as if it was their last, because it very well could have been.

Once their plates were clean, Waters offered them each a cigarette, wordlessly with a gesture of the open pack towards them. For once, they all decided to partake.

"Fuck me, man. I'm glad I quit, but something about this cigarette after that meal is like a cherry on top," Marquez said with a deep, heavy exhale of the smoke in his lungs. "The one when we first got here tasted like shit - I guess it was the fear - but this?" Marquez grunted with satisfaction.

Feig stared up at the ceiling, with the smoke gently leaving his nostrils. Miller twirled his cigarette between his ring and index fingers between drags. He was making sure he didn't smoke it too fast. They each finally pulled their respective last drags, all the way down to the filter, and snuffed the remaining flames on the ashtray in the middle of the table.

"Well, guys, it's about time I hit the bunks. If we all buy the farm, I just wanted to say it was a pleasure getting to know you a little, even if the circumstances are pretty shit," Marquez said in a serious tone, despite his intentionally comical choice of words.

Everyone gave a nod in agreement, and after a brief silence, stood up to head to their bunks.

***

"When plunder becomes a way of life for a group of men in a society, over the course of time they create for themselves a legal system that authorizes it and a moral code that glorifies it."
— Frédéric Bastiat

Chapter 3 - Stranger in A Strange Land

Date: January 7th, 2140
User: Oldenburg, Kirk
Time: 14:36:45

CONFIDENTIALITY NOTE: Pursuant to the Electronic Communications Privacy Act, 18 U.S.C. Sec. 2510 - 2522, the contents of this log and the attachments hereto (if any) are confidential, privileged, and/or otherwise exempt from disclosure and are intended only for disclosure to and use by the intended recipient of this message and ranking officials within the Department of Defense and/or Homeland Security. If you are not the intended recipient of this message, the receipt of this message is not intended to and does not waive any applicable confidentiality or privilege and you are hereby notified that any dissemination, distribution, printing or copying of the contents of this message is strictly prohibited. If you have received this transmission in error, please contact us or immediately reply to the sender that you have received this communication in error and delete it from your file server.

I just got the word that we're going to be mobilizing soon. China's troops landed in the U.K., and we're obligated to defend them. I'm not sure how that works, considering China practically owns our government with the amount of debt that we have, but that's above my pay grade. I've got the rest of the logistics team scrambling to procure as much weaponry as possible from our suppliers in the Middle East, and the mechanics are working three day shifts of eighteen hours a piece with one day off in between just to get the amphibs up to snuff for beach deployments.

In ten years in the armed forces, two deployments to Russia, and three to Somalia, I haven't seen this many people in an uproar. Even the commanders are frazzled. China went to shit after Hong Kong annexed themselves off from the mainland, and now they're desperate. Apparently, Khabarovsk and Vladivostok already fell, and we just got news of the attacks a few days ago.

If the rumors I'm hearing are true, they're also spearheading attacks on the southern tip of India and making their way to Saudi Arabia to block off any forces from the U.K. by sea from pincering them as they make their way through Russia. Kazakhstan went dark last night at 21:00. Whatever this move is, it has been years in the making, and I suspect we're not getting the full story. They have to have been getting help from somewhere, because I just can't see how they would be able to successfully tackle three separate fronts without being noticed. Luckily, my job isn't to ask questions, so I'm going to leave it. I just want you to know, that I miss you, and I love you, and I hope whatever this is doesn't turn into a full-scale war, but I doubt they would have moved me to the new Rose Cross installation if it wasn't serious.

Love, Kirk

***

Date: February 14th, 2140
User: Oldenburg, Kirk
Time: 03:16:22

I changed the header of my logs so you won't get that dumb confidentiality notice anymore. We know they're listening, it's fine. Anyway, I can't sleep much. These weeks without you have been brutal, and it doesn't look like the situation is getting any better. China and Mongolia apparently became a unified state without telling anybody. How the hell our intelligence division didn't realize that Mongolia had a standing army is beyond me, but that very army went and took the southern regions of Russia and Kazakhstan in their entirety, with the Chinese and Mongolian forces moving towards Ukraine and Belarus. The only action our forces have seen has been out to sea and in the air. You remember my buddy that was a pilot? Rick? He got shot down over the East China Sea. Luckily for him, the navy scooped him up before the Chinese destroyers made it out to bomb the wreckage. He's hurt pretty badly, but he'll live.

I miss you terribly. The videos we send back and forth are nice, but it just isn't the same. This drab base must have been painted with Depression Number 5, because it's miserable here. It feels like every other day the orders change. One day I'm procuring fuel and planning its delivery to our bases overseas, and the next it's getting building materials for the boats and tanks here in Philadelphia.

How's New York? Are the dogs eating okay? I'd pay a million bucks to have a few glasses of wine with you and shoot some bottles with the .22 out back, and watch some old movies like we used to. I know I'm good at planning the supply chain, but I miss you, Hyeon. I did my time already, I was going to retire! We both know that. I don't know, I'm just struggling. Are the townspeople treating you okay? They know you're Korean, right? I saw on the news last night that a bunch of Chinese restaurants got vandalized. I wish I could just blame it on fear, but these people have been Americans for generations. They may be Chinese by descent, but it's not like they're fucking spies or something. I'm sorry sweetheart, I know you don't like it when I curse, but I thought we were over this. It was bad enough when Roosevelt locked up Japanese citizens during the second World War, the last thing we need is more incensed politicians acting on fear and popularity to start putting anyone of Asian descent into camps.

I'm sorry, love, I don't mean to make you upset or afraid, but you know where the guns are and how to use them. If anyone tries to give you any trouble you send them on their merry way without making a fuss, okay? I can't imagine anyone from town giving you a hard time, but times of war changes people. I have to get some sleep dear, I know I keep saying it, but I miss you, and I love you. Please be safe, and make sure to rig that one window in the office that doesn't lock properly. Good night/good morning (whenever you get this).

All of my love, Kirk

***

Date: March 4th, 2140
User: Oldenburg, Kirk
Time: 18:01:50

The Chinese-Mongol army took their first steps in Finland. They're putting up a decent fight, but it's not looking good. The talking heads at the top still haven't deployed any of our troops, they're taking a "wait and see" approach, meanwhile hundreds of thousands have died so far already. I'm ready for this to all be over, not just so I can finally feel you in my arms again, but so all of this death and misery can end.

We've been working day and night on weapons, boats, and getting materials shipped to bases around the world. I think they're planning on deploying some soldiers soon. The messed-up thing is, I can't help but feel that if China wasn't so stubborn with their economy, they wouldn't have had to deal with that famine on their own. Sure, there were a few attempts at getting food over there, but the politicians - both domestic and foreign - shut them down in an instant. People wanted to help, and maybe if they were allowed to, we wouldn't be in this situation, but thinking about what-ifs makes my brain hurt.

We had an entire Panamax vessel with ten thousand TEU's of supplies get sunk off the coast of South Africa a few days ago. I got my ass chewed out, even though I wasn't the one that said "we don't have enough ships to escort the supplies, the Chinese won't be that far south." Regardless, I'm in the dog house for the time being, and I still just can't get you out of my mind.

I miss your kimchi. I hope you're still making it. We didn't spend a thousand dollars on earthenware crocks for nothing! The food here is terrible. They occasionally get us some decent food, but otherwise it's standard military rations. I thought I was tired of them before, but having tasted your food for so long and now being deprived of it, it truly has no flavor. It's like salted cardboard. I might have to resort to thievery to get some gochugaru flakes to put on the slop they're giving us. The first time you cooked for me, I knew I was going to marry you. I damn near ate myself to death the first time you made that huge spread of food. You had such a huge smile on your face because I enjoyed it so much, and you knew how damn good of a cook you were. I had to fight you for months to get you to say "yes," and it was a fight worth having. You thought I was coming after your business! Who would have thought that you would have needed such a handsome logistics expert? It really feels like it was all just yesterday... we were young kids, and you were already running the show with clothing distribution, meanwhile I was a lowly grunt who fell in love with a beautiful, caring woman. I had nothing to offer you then, and you still gave me a chance.

I hope you're not regretting that chance, my love. I know this time apart has to be hurting you too. I cried the other night, for the first time since you said "I do." I don't know how much more of this I can take. I was supposed to be out, and I'm furious that I've been away from you for so long. Kiss the dogs for me, and let them know daddy misses them.

Missing you desperately, Kirk

***

Date: April 19th, 2140
User: Oldenburg, Hyeon
Time: 10:29:05

Good morning, my dear. I wish I had good news for you, but you know better than anyone what's happening. The nationwide tax hike just took another forty percent of the company's earnings. I had to lay off three hundred employees just to be able to break even, and that doesn't even factor in what we're going to lose in sales now that people aren't spending as much anymore. I had to dip into our savings in order to cover the back taxes for the first month of the new tax rate. I know that was supposed to pay for our farm to retire on, but I had no other choice. I hope you understand.

I've still been making kimchi. I've been having my parents over more often to make sure it doesn't go to waste. Mom is worried about you, but I've done my best to keep her fears at bay. The dogs still wait by the door for you every night, and I have to hold back the tears as they cry when you don't come through the door. I know what you're doing is important, but forgive me for feeling selfish and wanting you all to myself.

I saw on the news that the Chinese army stepped foot in Poland, so I'm not expecting you home any time soon. What's keeping the U.S. from intervening? You said they were going to deploy troops soon. I need you at home.

It's been hard to maintain our relationship through video logs, but you know that I would wait an eternity for you. I'm tired of having an empty bed, and I know it's not your fault, my love, but I grow angrier by the day. I want my husband back. Write back soon, I miss you.

Love, Hyeon

***

Date: May 19th, 2140
User: Oldenburg, Kirk
Time: 09:34:40

Good morning my love. From what I can gather, they've got twelve different battalions getting ready to deploy, but there hasn't been any news of a date. From what I can tell, it could be as soon as July, or as late as next year. Everyone is confused and exhausted. We've been working so hard for so long now, that we can't seem to find any light at the end of the tunnel.

With China's footprint now covering almost all of Asia and bleeding into Europe, it's hard to estimate when they'll make their way into the U.K. Poland has kept them at bay with many bloody battles. The total death toll is up to over two million on all sides. They haven't reported it on the news, but there have been widespread rapes and executions in all of the countries the Chinese control.

One of my procurement officers, Cao Chanming, was found beaten to a pulp. He's in intensive care right now, but I can't figure out who did it. Every son of a bitch on base is covering for whoever it was. They think just because he's Chinese, he's a traitor, and quite frankly, it pisses me off. He's been one of my best guys for over five years, and he's sitting in the med bay bloodied and bruised. He's got internal bleeding for fucks sake. I'm sorry, I know, the cursing, but this man has done more for us than most, and to see him treated like this has me furious. I put in a request for a formal investigation to the matter, but I haven't heard anything except "we'll look into it". I'm beginning to wonder who the real enemies are... I have to go, Rose Cross is a madhouse as of late, and you never know who's looking over your shoulder. I love you, Hyeon.

Love, Kirk

***

Date: December 31st, 2140
User: Oldenburg, Kirk

Time: 23:52:16

It's almost the new year, and not being able to start it without you in my arms and your lips smashed against mine is killing me. I might have had a few to drink, but I'm okay, I promise. I'm not even supposed to be drinking, but I've got some electrolyte packs for the morning at least. The battalions are deploying tomorrow to Northern Ireland and England. If we don't make it happen here, then there's no stopping them. If I have to look at another supply chain presentation, I think I'm going to vomit. That is, if the whiskey doesn't do it first.

Tonight is the quietest night we've had on base in months. You'd think it would be the opposite, but with the U.S officially joining the war effort tomorrow, it's morose around here. Lots of us have friends or family that are going to the front lines. I feel bad that I get to sit in my office, but that's the job.

I tried to watch the New Year celebrations, but I can't take it seriously when the country is trying to pretend everything is okay when we have ten thousand soldiers about to see combat. I don't want to be a downer, but it's been over a year since I've seen you in person, and every day feels like it's getting longer. My nights are restless, and I can't shake this feeling that something is terribly wrong about this war. I never was the conspiracy type, but there are a lot of things not adding up.

To add insult to injury, they still haven't started an investigation into who put Chanming into a coma. He's alive, but he's wasting away every time I go to see him. His family is holding onto hope, and I am too, but no one knows if he's going to come out of it or not. If I had the means, I'd find out who did it myself. He didn't deserve that, and he sure as hell doesn't deserve to be on life support.

Stay safe, my love. Once we're officially taking part in this war, everything is going to change.

Love, Kirk

***

Date: January 11th, 2141
User: Oldenburg, Hyeon
Time: 08:29:37

I saw the news this morning. The first battalion landed in Portrush late evening on the 9th. They got completely wiped out. I'm scared, Kirk. When are you coming home?

There are anti-war protests and riots all over New York City, New Jersey, and Pennsylvania. The California protests got so out of hand that they've enacted martial law across the entire state. Rioters almost made it through the blockade to Rose Cross yesterday. If anything happened to you, I don't know what I'd do. Please just tell me you're okay and that this will all be over soon. The people in town are getting worried that the military is going to be setting up posts here in upstate New York to keep the people from fleeing the city to avoid being persecuted for crimes against the state. There could be criminals in our backyard, Kirk!

I've been practicing with the hand gun more, you always said it was my weak spot, and I don't want to have a weak spot with the way the country is going. The dogs finally stopped waiting by the door, but they still look around the house for you every morning.

I have some other news, but I don't quite know how to say it...

I'm going to have to close the business, Kirk. I had to lay off so many people and downsize to make up for the lack of revenue, but the tax rate leaves nothing left to run operations. The government keeps running ads that every dollar is spent on ensuring the war effort is successful, but all we've seen so far is millions of dead across the board, with almost a quarter of that being our own. People aren't happy, and it's not getting any better.

The president was in talks with the Canadian Prime Minister about a "mutually beneficial agreement." There haven't been many details, but we're hoping it's a trade agreement to help the economy, and maybe I can use the rest of our savings to restart what we once had. Mom hasn't stopped crying since I told her, she thinks we're doomed. I wish you were here to help calm her down, she always listened to you.

I know it's going to be hard, but we always came out on top of any challenges we faced, as long as we faced them together. We're going to be okay, right? Please come home soon. I can't take this much longer.

Missing you dearly, Hyeon.

***

Date: April 30th, 2141
User: Oldenburg, Kirk
Time: 00:19:42

Chanming passed away late last night. No investigation, not even a single question raised except for me. I'm done sitting around waiting for someone else to do the right thing. Maybe I'll get lucky and they'll discharge me for meddling. At least then I can finally be with you again.

I'm going to pull some strings with some of the network security guys, they owe me a few favors for keeping them here in the states. I'm going to find out who did this to him and I'm going to make sure they get what's coming to them. I got in touch with them shortly after he passed. None of this is adding up. They told me it may take a few days to get the information on a SecDrive, but once I get it, I'm going to send you a copy of whatever I have in case anything happens to me.

I'm so sorry to have to drag you into this, but what kind of man would I be if I could let atrocities like this go without justice? It's bad enough when murders happen in the streets, but if our own government is willing to turn a blind eye to murder, then someone needs to get the story out. Chanming's family deserves to know what happened, and they deserve to know that nothing was done about it. I'll be in touch in a few days on my private channel.

I love you, and I'm sorry.
-Kirk

***

Date: March 6th, 2141
Sender: kirk.oldenburg/freenet/vmessage
Timestamp: 11:27 AM EST

I don't have much time, so I'll be as brief as possible. I've attached the contents of my SecDrive, you need to get them out onto public channels as soon as possible. Chanming was murdered on orders that came from within the D.O.D., and the network guys dug up more. The military waited to engage on purpose, it wasn't "lack of readiness" or "lack of supplies", it was strategic. I don't know why, but they let the bloodshed happen while we sat here scrambling for what we thought was preparation. They could have engaged whenever they wanted.

When you publish the files, publish our conversations... The country, and the world, needs to know that I'm not a madman, and that you're nothing but a wonderful, supportive wife, who had the rotten luck of being married to me. Make it look accidental, there's a GDF file in there with instructions as well as a decryption tool so you can read it. Words can't express how sorry I am, my love, but we have to do this.

I have to lay low for a while, so I'm going to bury myself in work to not raise any suspicions. If we're lucky, I get a dishonorable discharge and some prison time, but we'll finally be together.

Tell your parents I miss them, and that I'm sorry. Hug the dogs for me, and give them extra treats for me. I said a while back that nothing was going to be the same. I hate being right. Something I rarely had to worry about when you were around.

I almost wish I didn't stick my nose into all of this... but he was a good man, and I had to watch his family grieve for him...

My parents used to tell me "It's not always easy doing what's right," and I carried that with me for my entire childhood and into my adult life. Here I am doing what's right, and it's dragging the person I love into what could only become a shit storm. I'm sorry, I know. We always got through anything, as long as we did it together.

Be in touch soon,

-Kirk

***

Date: June 29th, 2141
Sender: seo-hyeon.oldenburg/freenet/vmessage
Timestamp: 7:21 AM EST

I haven't heard from you in months, Kirk. I'm fearing for the worst, and my heart can't take it right now. Mom is sick, and our savings is dwindling away. The United States and Canada have some agreement that is completely flipping the healthcare industry on its head. We have to use the federally mandated providers, and since they're offering free care to everyone who can't afford it, our office visits are over three thousand dollars per visit.

I'm scared, Kirk. I read the files on the SecDrive. I don't know what the Petty Island base has to do with any of this, but delaying the fight was definitely on purpose. Two more battalions just landed in England, and they're saying that this is the "make it or break it" moment for the war.

They've enacted country wide curfews to keep protestors in check. Almost every state except a few have enacted martial law. The tax rate is sitting strong at eighty percent to fund the war, meanwhile everything else is starting to break down. Food is being rationed through a lottery and numbering system.

Businesses are closing, New York city is almost entirely shut down. The ports and shipping lines are all now federally operated. I'm glad you told me to keep making the kimchi a while back, because I've been living off of it on the weeks my number doesn't come up for food. The last time I got called, all I got was a pound of rice and a few ounces of chicken. I don't know what's going on Kirk, but it isn't good. Some of the people actually wanted this, while the rest are trying to fight back. I'm terrified and lonely.

Please respond to me soon, I can't bear it any longer.

Love, Hyeon

***

Date: July 21st, 2141
Sender: seo-hyeon.oldenburg/freenet/vmessage
Timestamp: 9:45 AM EST

The war is over, Kirk. When our forces successfully landed in England, the Chinese-Mongolian army was spread out so thin that they've surrendered, despite the long and bloody battle that took place there. The nations the Chinese marched through are seeking aid, and the government is planning a post-war tribunal to decide what China's punishment will be.

Canada, South America, and the United States are merging into an empire, "The Democratic Republic of the Americas". The president announced it this morning after declaring victory over the Chinese. Canada and all of South America will start learning English by next week. If they're not at a conversational level by next year, they'll be annexed from the DRA while simultaneously still be denied access to their natural resources. If they do, they'll be provided housing, food, healthcare, and jobs, but I'm not buying it. I didn't flee North Korea just to see it spread. They weren't there, they have no idea what kind of curse they're putting on these people. On us.

Remember the little girl I told you about when I still lived there? Her name was Kim Min-jung. Her parents were arrested for stealing meat because they had another baby on the way, and her mother was not doing well. She followed me around like a puppy, because I looked after her. We would do odd jobs to help people around the village and buy scraps from the food carts to stay fed. One day, we were resting in the shade, and she said to me "I feel tired, Seo-Hyeon" and she fell asleep on me. I was exhausted and went to sleep as well. I woke up a few hours later and noticed that she had vomited on both of us in her sleep. There were flies everywhere, and I was so angry at first. I shook her to wake her up, only she didn't wake up. She had passed away the moment she closed her eyes, and I stood there in the street, crying and wailing as loud as I could, but no one seemed to care. I had to leave her there in the street to go home. A few weeks later, my parents had saved enough to pay a smuggler to get us into China, and from China we were able to work and secure passage to America.

I know you hate that story. You hated to think of me having to live in such a way, or anyone, for that matter, but the reason I bring it up is that whatever this is, this Democratic Republic of the Americas... I can feel in my heart that it is going to be the same way, but for so many more people.

I don't know if you're even getting these messages anymore. I don't even know if you are alive. Everyone else from Rose Cross has returned home, and every day I wake up in anticipation to see you walk through that door, and every day my heart breaks again.

With this message, I will have done what you asked. The world will see what is truly happening without the wool being pulled over their eyes. I don't regret marrying you, Kirk. You said I had rotten luck for being married to you, and I'm going to stay mad at you until you take it back. Everything we had, everything we shared, was worth it.

Farewell, Kirk.
Love, your angry wife, Seo-Hyeon.

***

The screens across the country all cut to the evening report on the Federal News Network. The anchor Carl Wilson sat upright, front and center, with a saddened look across his face, which he was desperately trying to mask.

"Good evening, ladies and gentlemen, it is August eighteenth at nine o' clock Eastern Time. We're interrupting your usual broadcasting for an important development. Earlier this afternoon, the source of the falsified documents that were released to the public a week ago has been found. Forty-three-year-old Seo-Hyeon Oldenburg, CEO of Ultimax Clothing, a once popular clothing line, and wife of Kirk Oldenburg, was the distributor of these documents. Kirk, if you recall from our broadcast last week, was the Director of Logistics for the Department of Defense, who vanished mysteriously from his post at the Rose Cross military base in Philadelphia.

Intelligence agents were able to track down missus Oldenburg by using a brute force decryption method that revealed traces of garbage data within the messages that she and her husband exchanged over the past year or so, most of which was irrelevant, but the scrubbed header data points to both Kirk and Seo-Hyeon Oldenburg actively inciting dissent among the masses with lies against the state. Kirk falsified the documents and passed them to his wife, who distributed it broadly on all public networks. The Secretary of Defense has labeled them as domestic terrorists, and the Department of Justice has given her a sentence of... public execution.

Ladies and gentlemen, if you have small children watching, please have them leave the room, as the imagery we're about to show is going to be live and extremely graphic. For the first time in almost two hundred years, the United States government will be executing, publicly, Seo-Hyeon Oldenburg for treason and inciting violence. I repeat, if you have small children, please have them leave the room."

The camera switched to Seo-Hyeon, bound and crying on her knees with a group of soldiers lined up behind her. The Secretary of Defense walked on screen and approached a podium.

"It brings me great sadness that a citizen of this beautiful country, where freedom and prosperity are key to our values, would perform such a heinous and treasonous act. To betray one's own country is to betray one's own brothers and sisters. This great land allowed her to open her business, and to succeed for so many years. When this country asked for a small favor in return to ensure that our sons and daughters didn't die in vain fighting off the Chinese-Mongolian threat, to aid our brothers-in-arms in Europe, she took it upon herself to spit in the face of her protectors. Without our laws, there would be chaos. Without our armies, we would be weak. Without our generosity, we would starve. Without order, there is only destruction and death. You chose us to represent you, and to do what must be done for the greater good. We cannot allow terrorism on our own soil to tarnish our good name, and to incite fear in our free citizens.

By the powers vested in the Department of Justice, I shall hereby carry out their sentence, to the maximum extent of the law. Execution by firing squad. In the name of justice, missus Oldenburg, you have been sentenced to death. Do you have any final words?"

The camera zoomed in on her face, her eyes puffed and red from the endless stream of tears that had rolled down her cheeks. She looked directly into the camera and began to speak, her lips quivered with fear and anxiety.

"My husband and I are not traitors. Nothing I released was falsified, we only wanted you to all know the truth. They are not your protectors, and they are not your benefactors! They killed my husband, and now they're going to kill me. I love you, Kirk. I did as you asked. I'll see you soon, my love."

Shortly after she finished, the Secretary of Defense looked over at the soldiers in a line and gave a nod. Like clockwork, they raised their rifles to their shoulders. The soldier in the middle began to shout his orders.

"On my mark! One! Two! Three! Fire!"

She didn't flinch. Her eyes remained open even after the guns began to fire. Her body jolted violently as each round pierced her flesh. The life began to drain from her eyes, and screams of terror were heard across the nation. Her body laid motionless for a few seconds, and she attempted to speak with her last ounce of strength. The middle soldier unholstered a pistol and placed a bullet in the back of her head, which thumped heavily on the ground.

The camera switched back to Carl Wilson, who signed off with a tear in his eye and a tremor in his voice.

"Good night... ladies and gentlemen. Godspeed to you all. I'm Carl Wilson, reporting from the Federal News Network in Washington D.C."

***

"Tu ne cede malis, sed contra audentior ito." [Do not yield to evils, but proceed ever more boldly against them]
— Virgil, The Aeneid

Chapter 4 - Déjà vu

The klaxon blared loudly, which pierced their ears and roused the prisoners from their sleep.

"What the fuck? It's not even six am!" Waters shouted, trying to overcome the loudness of the alarm.

The commander's voice boomed over the speaker system, "This is not a drill, gentlemen, get to the armory and gear up. We've got movement from the Manticore and you'll be deploying immediately."

They hurriedly ran out of the bunks, through the mess hall, and up the stairs to the catwalk. They were half awake but their hearts pounded with anxiety as they sped towards the armory, rattling the catwalk violently as they went. As they approached the armory entrance, the door flung open with Schuck standing in the doorway.

"Come on, get geared up! We've gotten everything ready for you. I'll do my best to explain while you're getting ready." His voice was uncharacteristically panicked, which concerned the group. They each scrambled to get into their armor, Feig finished first with his slow and meticulous approach. Waters had his chest armor on backwards at first and cursed himself while he spun it around on his torso to straighten it out. Miller's eyes were drooped as he slid his gauntlets on and grabbed his gloves. Marquez stumbled with one foot on the floor as he tried to slide on his other boot.

"Gentlemen, we haven't seen movement like this from the Manticore this close to daylight ever. We're going to take this as an opportunity to deploy you to the maintenance hatches to track it and see if you can bring it down. You'll have approximately two and a half hours of time to interact before it ultimately goes back into hiding. We don't know why it's so active in the main areas of the sub level, but the only variable we have that could have contributed is the fact that you've been patrolling the island and it was actively following you underground. It's a slim lead, but a lead nonetheless. We've already activated your combat sensors in your helmets, so we'll be getting a live feed from all of you. If we get any relevant information, we'll pass it along over the comms quietly or directly to your HUDs."

"We haven't eaten yet, man!" Waters exclaimed.

"Luckily, by the time the Manticore goes back into hiding, breakfast will be ready for you, so let that be your motivation if you must, but you have to get going. Grab your weapons and get moving!" Schuck retorted smugly.

Marquez took the standard issue rifle and pistol as well as flash grenades, cryogenic grenades, and multiple magazines of ammunition. Miller followed suit. Waters took a rifle and a shotgun. Feig stuck to a handgun for his weapon, but also grabbed a net launcher, stun mines, smoke grenades, and a modified tranquilizer rifle. The gear felt familiar to everyone, but they were told the ammunition for each was purposefully crafted for this encounter.

Schuck activated the comms microphone on his lapel and radioed ahead to the gate, "Open the gate, they'll be there by the time it's open."

Marquez and Waters sharply turned their heads to Schuck, who had the slightest grin on his face. "I suggest you all get going."

Without a word, the group looked at each other, as if to sigh all at once, and sprinted out of the open door.

"Shouldn't have had that cigarette" Marquez said in between breaths.

"No regrets!" Waters exclaimed shortly before gasping for air.

The low branches by the catwalk clicked and clacked against their armor as they ran through them, causing the branches to swing violently back and forth.

"All this tech and they couldn't hire a fucking gardener?" Waters said with a chuckle, breathing very heavily at full sprint.

Their armor rattled as they descended the stairs. They heard the hiss of the hydraulics from the main gate, which was almost completely open. The guard operating the gate gave them a welcoming wave through the gate, much like a butler would, and smiled as the four flung through the gate. The guard hit the switch to close it, and peeked in to give the group a wave and a smile, but only Marquez and Miller were looking back at the gate.

***

"Alright guys, pull the map up on your HUDs, and get your flashlights on. We're going to head towards the hatch that Miller found. Step quietly and with intent. Keep voice chatter to a minimum until we get there. Feig, your hearing seems to be the best, so keep an ear to the ground to see if you can hear the Manticore trailing us again, or if you can hear it at all. Sound good?" Marquez said in a slightly hushed voice.

"Sounds good to me, boss," Waters responded.

"Boss?" Marquez said, puzzled. "I'm just trying to make sure you assholes get out alive."

Feig smirked, and Miller looked at Marquez with a subtle nod of approval.

They began their trek through the thick trees and controlled their steps in order to make as little noise as possible. Feig walked with his right hand on the grip of his pistol, and his left hand clutched in a fist, hovering just in front of his left leg. Waters was scanning their field of view left to right, over and over again, looking for anything out of the ordinary. Miller's right index finger sat straight across the trigger housing, with the barrel of his rifle pointing towards the ground. *Miller must not be expecting any action here on the surface*, Marquez thought, *but Waters is ready for anything. I can't blame him, the guy has literally been through hell, and here we are in another circle of it.*

Feig threw his left fist in the air, his arm making a right angle, signaling the team to stop. Everyone stopped in their tracks, and the woods were completely quiet. Marquez looked at his HUD and saw that the hatch was about fifty-five meters away. Feig crouched down on the ground and listened intently. The silence permeated their ears. Only a high-pitched squeal and gentle, controlled breathing sound reached the inside of their helmets. Then they heard that familiar sound. A low, dull thumping came from their right. Feig quickly adjusted the map on his HUD to find the approximate location of the sound and mark it on everyone's map. It was either in the main areas, or possibly in the maintenance hatch they were about to enter.

"What should we do, guys? Maintenance hatch or elevator down?" Marquez whispered into the communicator.

"It's hard to tell. Since it's moving, it could be in either spot," Feig responded in a hush.

Waters looked at the marker on his map and thought deeply, his breathing got a little faster and a little harder. Adrenaline was beginning to pump through his veins, as he was already imagining their encounter with the Manticore. Sweat beaded on his forehead.

"Waters, you okay?" Marquez whispered.

"Yeah, yeah. Sorry... I say we go in through the hatch and make our way to the elevator. We can make a good sweep, and we'll finish by the exit to safety."

"Copy that, everyone else on board?"

Miller and Feig nodded in agreement.

Waters, Miller, and Feig formed a semicircle around the hatch, and Marquez crouched down to uncover the handle. He twisted the handle and pulled it up until it clicked into position. A short, but high-pitched loud burst of compressed air escaped from the hydraulics of the hatch. Feig winced at the sound, worried that it alerted the creature to their position.

Marquez climbed down first. The maintenance halls were cramped and pitch black. The dank, mildewy smell couldn't be filtered out by the rebreather in his helmet, and he unintentionally made a disgusted grunt at the offensive odor. *Fuck me,* he said in his mind. He reached his right hand up to a button on the side of his visor that turned on the adaptive night vision mode. He looked up to the group and waved his hand for the next one to come down. Marquez checked left and right, bordering on panicked, while Waters descended and flipped on his night vision. He waved to Feig, but Miller was already getting onto the ladder. Once Miller got to the bottom, Feig looked up to the sky. He saw rain drops land on his visor, and he let out a deep sigh before he got onto the ladder and pulled the hatch shut behind him.

The sound of the rain on the ground above them got louder. The rain was pouring harder and harder each minute that passed by. It reminded them of their arrival on the rainy boat ride just a few days ago. Waters scanned their perimeter and saw the labyrinthine layout of the maintenance tunnels first hand.

"How the hell are we supposed to navigate this?" Waters whispered.

"Feig, can you set up our maps? Add the position of the sound we heard if you can," Marquez said.

"I can try, but the heavy rain is going to obscure the audio, and plus it probably moved since then."

"Copy that, we'll use it as a point of reference regardless. Watch your corners, and don't open any doors without a team mate," Marquez said sternly.

Small pools of water were scattered about the cramped halls, built up from water that had trickled in over the years. Trails of water pouring in ran down the sides of the walls, with roots that protruded through parts of the ceiling. They continued to step quietly, trying to avoid larger puddles and making splashes. Miller and Feig watched the rear, while Waters slung his rifle over his shoulder and grabbed his shotgun. He was preparing for a close quarters encounter. Marquez watched straight ahead and scanned, constantly looking at the map in his helmet.

The group came across an intersection, with the left path heading directly towards the main offices, and the right path going farther around, behind some of the offices and restrooms on the perimeter of the sub level.

"Should we split up? Two and two?" Marquez asked.

"Are you fucking kidding me? Haven't you ever watched any of the old movies? The second they split up is when they get picked off one by one. Screw that, strength in numbers. Feig and Miller keep watching the rear, we watch the front. Pick a direction," Waters responded, flabbergasted at the suggestion.

Miller laughed, but apologized for it, "I'm sorry, I know this is serious, but come on Joey, even I wasn't going to suggest that."

"Let's go left. We can follow that artery straight for about a hundred meters, then bear left and we can use the access panel to get into the executive offices. Wide open spaces, and we'll have a straight shot to the elevator," Feig said coldly.

"Don't have to tell me twice, let's go," Marquez said bashfully, after getting reprimanded for unintentionally trying to set the group up to get killed.

Marquez swiftly moved to the other side of the corridor, while Waters stayed on the side closest to Feig and Miller. They looked down the hall intently, searching for disturbances and listening for signs of movement. Feig and Miller looked down the path they opted not to go down. He wanted to make sure they didn't get attacked from behind. Their adaptive night vision sensors could only do so much, and eventually the hall turned to pitch black. Marquez and Waters looked at each other, gave a quick nod, and began to slowly step down the hallway, with Feig and Miller following behind.

They were halfway down the hall when they heard a loud banging, but couldn't place how close or far it was. Everyone raised their weapons and readied their trigger fingers, straight across the trigger housing, ready to fire at a moment's notice. A clearly audible growl resonated through the walls, it was like a combination of a howl, growl, and shriek all at once. It was sharp and piercing, but also deep and rumbling.

"Where the fuck is it?" Waters said anxiously.

"I-I can't place it exactly, but it looks like it's near the cafeteria, a few yards down the hall from the executive offices," Feig responded with a slight stutter.

"Let's move quickly," Marquez said, starting to move faster. "It probably already heard us. We need to get into position." He finished his sentence as the whole group started to move at a brisk jog towards the access panel. Their boots made splashing thuds in the small puddles, while the heavy rain above still resounded through the ceilings, like static in the distance.

They arrived at the access panel and formed a small perimeter around it. Feig tried to turn the access handle but it was rusted and seized into place.

"Feig. Access panel? Please?" Waters said with urgency.

"I'm trying, it's rusted. Everybody, stand back."

"Why? Just ope-" Waters tried to interrupt.

"Just stand back, now! You've got five seconds!"

Waters and Marquez peeled off to the left, Feig grabbed Miller and pulled him to the right. A low beep went off five times, followed by a small, controlled explosion.

"Ah, breaching charge. See? This is why I keep him around" Waters said with a nervous laugh.

"Waters, you're with me. Feig and Miller, you go counter clockwise. Get a perimeter of the offices before we head out into the main hallway. Watch your fucking corners, and listen for movement in the maintenance halls or vents or anywhere you think it could come from. We don't really know what this thing is capable of," Marquez said with urgency.

The team nodded in agreement and began their perimeter sweep. The emptiness of the offices was eerie. It looked like the people that used to be there had simply vanished in an instant. Papers and folders left on the desks as if they were waiting for someone to come back and finish the work they were doing. Chairs were rolled back a few feet from their companion desks. Computers and interfaces were exactly where they belonged, yet somehow completely out of place. The screens were all off, but they weren't damaged. The two groups reconvened at the door. Marquez looked at Miller and Feig and slowly grabbed the handle to the door. He gently pulled the handle down and violently thrust the door open. Marquez and Waters hugged the left side of the doorway with Feig and Miller hugging the right. Each team checked the direction they came out for signs of the creature but saw nothing.

They carefully stepped around the corner to see some of the doors were ripped off of their hinges. Some of the furniture was scattered in the hallway, in multiple pieces. They heard that awful growl once again, and this time it sounded closer and clearer than before.

Before anyone could react, the hallway filled with dust. A loud crash filled the small corridor, and the sound of rubble tumbling to the ground echoed. The dust cloud interfered with their night vision temporarily, all they could see was a bright, muddled, amorphous figure. As the dust began to settle, Feig saw two bright objects down the hall. He knew after a few seconds of looking, that it was the creature.

It was the Manticore.

The briefings did it no justice, its size was immense, nearly filling the entire hallway. The hole in the wall that it broke through was as wide as three or four men, with splinters of broken wall where the sharp quills jutting out of its carapace broke through. When he looked back at the creature, he could see the tail, its chitinous end dripping with viscous toxin. The Manticore started to charge through the broken furniture and rubble, letting out its distinctive piercing growl.

Without hesitation, Waters crouched down and began firing his shotgun. The sound of the blast would have been deafening, but the sound dampeners in their helmets softened the blow. Marquez followed suit, crouching next to Waters and firing his rifle at the fast-moving beast. Feig scrambled to get his pistol in position and began to fire at gaps between its thickened skin patches. Miller grabbed a cryogenic grenade and armed it, throwing it fiercely towards its large, gaping maw. The explosion sprayed nitrogen gel all over the hallway, covering the debris in front of them. A frosty mist began to form from the heat and humidity rapidly melting the newly formed ice on the frozen rubble. The creature slowed for a moment, let out two quick shrieks, and took off in the opposite direction.

"Jesus Christ... it barely even flinched. Schuck are you listening? The thing barely even flinched!" Marquez said over comms.

"Pursue it now! The fact that it even retreated in the middle of conflict is something we've never observed here yet! Pursue it!" Schuck said angrily.

"Are we really taking orders from this asshole?" Waters said indignantly.

"It's our only way out of here. We've got it on the run. Feig, get the net gun ready. Waters, reload. Miller, get another cryo ready and let's go!"

The group took off to follow the Manticore, with Waters reloading on the run and Miller readying his cryogenic grenade. Feig holstered his pistol and took the net gun from his back, sliding back a large handle to arm it for launch. They slowed down as they approached the corner and listened for footsteps. They heard the creature fumbling around, but it didn't sound as if it was moving as fast as before. Marquez gave a hand signal and everyone poured around the corner ready to engage. The creature turned around and shrieked, scaring Miller, who in his fright armed the cryogenic grenade prematurely and dropped it to the floor.

"Fuck! I dropped it!" Miller squealed.

"Get rid of it, Miller!" Marquez scolded.

Miller fumbled around trying to grab the grenade before it exploded. He finally got a grip and threw it as best he could while in a half-crouched position. The grenade blew up a few feet in front of them, blinding their visors and creating a layer of frost on their armor.

"Shit, use your suits!" Marquez said.

They each hurried to press a button near the right hip on their armor that engaged climate control in their powered suits. After about thirty seconds, their suits and weapons were able to defrost, but the creature was nowhere in sight.

"FUCK! We lost it, and there's another intersection ahead," Waters said with deep breaths between every few words, as the group sprinted in the direction they last saw it.

"Behind! Behind!" Feig yelled.

The Manticore had ducked into an office on the side and let them run right past it. The creature was closer than ever and Miller didn't have another grenade ready. Waters opened fire immediately, striking the beast in a large, thick plate along its shoulder area. The creature stumbled for a second and continued to charge. Miller and Marquez opened fire to slow the creature down while Feig aimed the net gun at the center of its head, hoping to encapsulate its thundering legs, gaping maw, and deadly tail.

"Net now! Net!" Waters yelled over the comms. Feig hesitated. The net gun wasn't lined up properly with his shoulder and would have been inaccurate. He quickly hoisted the net gun to rest in between his shoulder and collar bone and pulled the large two finger trigger. The pressure from the compressed nitrous knocked him to the ground. The net got caught on a piece of reinforcement steel that was jutting out of one of the many damaged walls in the hallway and swung around violently. The creature proceeded past it and reared up to attack. Waters ran towards it and placed the barrel of his shotgun directly on the creature's chest area and pulled both triggers, firing two shots at once directly into its hardened husk.

The creature shrieked in agony and began to retreat once again.

Feig screamed in anguish, "My shoulder! I blew my fucking shoulder out!"

"We need to go after it!" Marquez yelled.

"I'm not leaving him, if that's what you're suggesting!" Waters said defiantly.

"Fine, get him up and follow when you can, let's go Miller!"

Miller looked at Marquez distressed. *He doesn't want to follow me. Why would he? It could be certain death for all I know. But we need to get out of here. All of us. It's heading towards the elevator,* Marquez thought.

"I'll stay on it, you three, rally up and meet me at the elevator!"

"Joey, come on!" Miller responded.

Marquez hesitated. "Meet me at the elevator!" he yelled as he leapt up and sprinted as fast as he could towards the elevator.

Marquez heard Waters chewing him out in the distance as he ran, "Fuckin' hero bullshit, you'll get all of us killed!"

He stopped around the corner when he saw the elevator. There was a reception room directly across from it, and he saw what looked like a human foot being dragged into the office. *I have to be seeing shit,* he thought, *either it's feeding on someone or there's someone else down here... No, no way.*

He ran as fast as he could, but he was exhausted from the endeavor so far. The powered armor helped him maintain stamina and shared some of the workload, but could only work in short bursts with internal power. He arrived at the door to the office and gazed in. There was a hole in the ceiling with daylight burning through. Not a lot, but clearly it was approaching morning daylight. He only noticed it for a second, because what he saw in the corner of the room was what looked like a naked woman.

"Are you okay?" he said, extending a hand and lowering his rifle.

She looked back at him with terror in her eyes, let out a piercing shriek and began to convulse wildly. Her limbs stretched and grew, large plates began to form around her body, and in less than ten seconds, he stood there, staring into the eyes of the Manticore. It let out two short shrieks and charged forward. Marquez tried to grab his rifle, but got plowed down to the ground. The creature took off away from the elevator, where Miller, Waters, and an injured Feig were waiting. Marquez looked over and tried to holler at Waters, who was readying his weapon.

"Don't shoot!" he screamed, but it was too late.

Waters fired three rapid shotgun blasts into the beast's side. It fell to the ground for a second, then leapt up and swiped with one of its sharp claws towards the group. Out of instinct, Miller and Waters dove out of the way. The beast continued running down the hallway until it was no longer in sight.

Marquez gathered himself and limped over to the elevator, picking up Miller from the ground. Waters got himself up and ran over to Feig.

"No... No! No no no no no no! FUCK! Schuck, we need a medic NOW!" Waters bellowed over comms.

"We'll have a team ready at the elevator, you need to get to the surface now," Schuck responded.

Miller pulled the switch to open the elevator and pulled Feig inside. His chest was clawed open, and he was bleeding rapidly. Feig's eyes became glassy and his breathing slowed. Waters clenched his rifle and stared into the hallway, biting down so hard his teeth hurt.

"I know you're angry, and I know you're going to want revenge, but going in by yourself isn't going to do anyone any good. We need to get him out of here and get him patched up. We need to get back, and we need to talk. For now, let's get the fuck out of here," Marquez said, with his hand placed on Waters' shoulder.

Waters brushed his hand away and rushed into the elevator to sit with Feig. He grabbed Feig's right arm and activated the adrenal stimulant package built into his suit. Feig jolted upright with a deep groan.

"Am I dead? What the fuck?" Feig said in a panic.

"You're in shock buddy, but you're not dead yet. There are medics waiting for you at the top, I'm not letting anything happen to you buddy, I promised, remember?" Waters said with a lump in his throat.

"Great job you're doing, pal," Feig responded with a blank expression, lightly gesturing to his torso with his right hand.

Waters laughed with tears in his eyes as the doors of the elevator opened and the bright rising sun blinded them all. A group of four medics lifted Feig and placed him onto a gurney. They rolled the gurney onto a medical truck and gestured the other three to get in. The six or seven steps it took to get into the truck felt like hours for Marquez, who was still dumbfounded by what he saw. *Am I going fucking insane? Either this thing is a girl, or it can mimic one*, he pondered anxiously.

No one said a word on the ride back. The medics removed Feig's helmet and arm gauntlets to be able to hook him up to the equipment in the truck. They put a rebreather on him to control his respiration and another medic began sanitizing the gashes across his chest. The medic opposite hooked him up to an IV to supply his body with hydration and nutrients for reforming the countless red blood cells he had already lost. After his wounds were sanitized, the medic applied a synthetic skin mesh to the wounds that looked like sheetrock tape, and applied a coagulant gel on top of it. Waters watched their every move with concern like that of a parent. The truck stopped and the back doors opened. Two medics at the med bay pulled out the gurney and the four on board got off to go with them. Waters got up to follow, but a guard stopped him.

"This isn't your stop, you'll be able to see him once the doctors are done with him, okay?" the guard said, trying to placate him.

Waters said nothing and sat back down. The doors shut and the truck drove for again what felt like hours, but in reality, was a mere few minutes. The truck once again came to a stop, and the doors opened.

"What are we doing at the mess hall?" Miller said.

Marquez was still lost in a thousand-mile stare. Waters looked puzzled.

Schuck appeared at the back of the truck, "I figured you would all want to eat since you missed breakfast. Perhaps fill up before the debriefing?"

"Forgive me if my appetite isn't quite there since I just watched my friend get mauled by a fucking six-foot-tall elephant wolf!" Waters said angrily, with bits of spit flying from his mouth.

"My apologies, mister Waters. Shall we proceed directly for debriefing?"

"Oh, come on, you're the science guy. You're supposed to be smart. Why would you have us debrief when you're missing a quarter of those who were there, dipshit?"

"Hm. Valid point. I'm not sure what it is that you want, but you can all get off here, and eat if you choose. If not, feel free to get some rest in your bunks or the mess hall. I had the requisitions officer set aside some more cigarettes for you, since they seem to be helping you relax. For what it's worth, I'm glad you all made it out."

No one responded to Schuck. They piled out and sat on the ground, leaned up against the wall next to the door to the mess hall. Waters pulled out his mangled pack of cigarettes with just a few remaining in it. He pulled off his helmet and threw it on the ground next to him. The blue flame of the butane lit the tip of the crooked cigarette. He breathed deep, and let out a whimper as he exhaled the smoke from his lungs. He handed the pack and lighter to Marquez who took one without hesitation. Miller took one as well. They sat there and smoked without a word for fifteen minutes.

***

The ash on Waters' cigarette was over two inches long. He stared blankly, barely moving a muscle. The thin wisps of smoke danced in a gentle upward helix for a few seconds more until fading out completely.

"Let's get this over with. Then we can go check on Feig," Marquez said, shattering the silence.

Miller and Waters got up without saying anything. Their faces were drained and pale. Fear, disbelief, and anger overcame them all at once, and yet they were only able to convey the disbelief. The shock had taken their tongues, and they slowly traipsed about, and headed towards the commander's office. The trees were still, and the thumps of the catwalk were dull shadows of their previous selves, stifled by the prisoners' exhaustion and apathy. After the short trip along the catwalk, they arrived back at the command center and filed into Wilkins' office.

"Gentlemen, before you say anything, just know that from what the medics are saying, mister Feig is going to make a full recovery. It'll take a few days to get him back on his feet, but you pulled yourselves out of there just in time," Wilkins preempted an uproar, but was surprised that he got no response. Waters' fists and teeth clenched with rage, but he didn't let out a peep. Wilkins grabbed a cigar out of his case with his leather clad right hand while his left hand fished around in his breast pocket, ultimately revealing a cutter. He snipped the end of his cigar off, fished back in his breast pocket and pulled out his butane lighter, igniting the bright blue flames and gently moving it from side to side in front of the tip of the cigar as he pulled in air, causing it to glow bright orange. He began to cough and wheeze, and sat down, resting the newly lit cigar in the ornate ash tray on his desk.

"Have a seat," he said politely, "let me pour you all a drink." He turned around in his chair and opened up an ice bucket on a small piece of mahogany furniture behind him. He placed three cold stones in a glass for each of them. He then took the decorative stopper out of a crystal decanter and poured the clear brown liquid into the glasses. He slowly turned his chair back around, holding a tray with four crystal tumblers filled two thirds of the way up with the brown liquid gently rocking back and forth. He placed the tray on his desk, covering the screen, and took each glass, one at a time, and placed it in front of Waters, Miller, and Marquez respectively. "It's not a particularly old or expensive scotch, but it gets the job done and it's not too sweet. Go ahead, drink up."

The prisoners looked at each other with hesitation, unsure if there was some sort of catch. Marquez gave a short, slight shrug and took a sip. He let out a small sigh as the scotch warmed his throat. Waters stared into the clear, dark brown liquid and watched his reflection shiver in the ripples. With a sharp exhale, he fired back the entire glass in one movement and slammed the glass down onto the desk with a thud. Miller jumped at the sound and spilled some of the scotch down the side of his glass and onto himself.

"We've had our analysts looking at the combat data you all gathered during your encounter with the Manticore. The special ammunition we gave you was technically successful, but clearly it wasn't quite enough to keep it down long enough to get a containment team in to secure it. You may look at this as a failure, but your excursion was the most success we've had since we've begun trying to capture it," Wilkins said in a serious tone.

"Of course you see it as a success! We're the fuckin' guinea pigs! Meanwhile Feig is in a med bay that we're not allowed into with a fuckin' gash across his chest that makes the shit I saw during the war look like child's play!" Waters interjected.

"First, I can assure you that mister Feig is going to recover. The medical team is applying the best practices in treatment to him and we're also gathering extremely useful data from it that may result in improved tech to defend against it, so while it's... regrettable that your friend had to suffer such an attack, you can't deny the usefulness of it. Silver linings and all, right?" Wilkins paused and glanced quickly at the unamused faces in front of him. "Secondly, you don't have to fret about another deployment any time soon. Your team's success was banked entirely on the four of you being in top shape. You won't be going back into the sublevels until Feig is back in fighting shape."

"Are you fucking kidding me?! It's bad enough I have to take orders from you, Chuck, and every other poor bastard with a boot in his mouth in this building, but I have to watch my friend get nearly clawed to death and just sit around with a thumb up my ass? You motherfuckers took everything from me. You took my wife, my kids, my livelihood, and you almost took the last fucking thing I have!" Waters stood up and yelled in anger.

"Hey, HEY! Relax man, let's jus-" Marquez tried to calm him down.

"Fuck this, and fuck all of you! I'm out of here," Waters stormed out, slamming the door behind him.

"It's alright. Tensions are high, but you all still understand your purpose here and the only way you're leaving, so," Wilkins poured himself another scotch, "keep that in mind. In a few weeks, mister Feig should be back up to snuff, and we'll have had plenty of time to analyze the combat data and make any modifications to the ammunition for your next encounter. Head to the cafeteria, get something to eat, and get some sleep. We'll have some exercises to keep you all on your toes while Mr. Feig recovers. Take the rest of that bottle with you too, would you? Doctor says I have to ease up on the ticker."

Marquez grabbed the bottle, stood up, gave Wilkins a slight smirk, and left with Miller in tow. As they were leaving headquarters and making their way towards the cafeteria and bunks, Marquez paused.

"Did you hear that?" he said with a scared excitement.

"Hear what?" Miller responded.

"That voice... I could have sworn I heard a voice coming from the ground! Listen!"

They stood silent for a minute.

"I still didn't hear nothing, Joey. You've been hitting that bottle pretty hard, and we had a pretty fucked up day. Let's just head back."

"Right..." Marquez responded.

There's a survivor down there, his mind raced, *either a survivor or another guinea pig like us... who was that girl?*

***

"Any number of scoundrels, having money enough to start with, can establish themselves as a 'government'; because, with money, they can hire soldiers, and with soldiers extort more money; and also compel general obedience to their will."
— Lysander Spooner

Chapter 5 - Brave New World

He couldn't open his eyes, but he could hear the shuffling of feet and equipment. He heard the beeping of monitors and the whirring of tools. He felt the sharp coldness of gel being applied to his skin, but he couldn't move. He knew he was breathing, but he couldn't breathe himself. He could feel the tube in his throat. He wanted to gag, but couldn't. Their voices sounded muffled, and he couldn't make out any of the words, but he heard their tone and heard the conviction and seriousness in their hushed voices.

Am I dead? Am I about to be dead? Feig thought, *I want to scream, but I can't. I hear them buzzing around me, but trying to lift a finger feels impossible right now. What have they drugged me up with? I need to talk to the guys. I need to talk to Waters... about what happened down there.*

The medical team continued to scramble around the operating table, the hum of the monitors was barely audible over the sound of countless nurses, scientists, and surgeons moving about the room. The scientists sat secluded in a back corner of the room, painstakingly going over charts and comparing them to combat schematics and data mined from the group's encounter with the Manticore. The surgeons had their assistants wiping sweat from their brows as they worked hurriedly, their surgical machines swapped out blades for clean ones, as the bloodied blades slowly sank to the bottom of sterilization tanks for re-use later.

Was I hurt that bad? That... thing scratched me up good, but they put a mesh on the wound, didn't they? Christ, it hurts.

The surgeon gestured to one of the nurses who brought over a small metallic object that resembled a large emerald. The surgeon placed it into the grips of a machine that hummed and whirred as it meticulously placed it into an incision in Feig's chest. The machine moved in such small increments they were almost imperceptible. Once it had the metallic object in place, it began to hum loudly as four screwdrivers began to spin, screwing the metal in place, and bonding together the part of Feig's sternum which had split in two.

The scientists took a moment to get out of their corner of the room and pull one of the surgeons to the side. He couldn't hear what words they were muffling, but the scientists sounded concerned, while the surgeon seemed standoffish.

Guess the nerds got told to mind their business. I wish these lab coats would mind theirs, what did they put in me? My chest feels like it's on fire. If I make it out of this, I can't say I'm optimistic for the future. Christ, isn't it bizarre that even though it's our own mind we still talk to it as if it's another person? Whatever they have me on must be good, I'm rambling like a madman. I'm not awake, yet I feel like I need to sleep.

***

"Yo, Waters, let me get a smoke," Marquez said, extending his hand.

Waters pulled the pack from his chest pocket and pulled a cigarette out and handed it over to Marquez, who then patted his pockets - side, rear, and chest - looking for a lighter. Waters already knew.

"You need a lighter too, I've got you. I think I'm going to join you anyway," Waters said as they began walking to the door leading outside of the mess hall. "Where's Miller? I haven't seen him since breakfast."

"He's over at the gym, believe it or not."

"No shit? Christ, this place must really be getting to him."

"Technically, it's gotten to all of us," Marquez said, slightly muffled by his lips being slightly separated with the cigarette hanging from his mouth. Waters lit his cigarette and held the lighter in the air with his right hand. Marquez took the lighter and struck it three times until it finally lit.

Waters was silent and stared into the distance.

"I'm sure he's alright, that wound was serious so he probably needs a lot of work, but he'll be back. Like Wilkins was saying, they want the whole team, so they're not going to let anything happen to him," Marquez said as smoke left his nostrils.

"You know exactly why I don't buy that bullshit. At the same time, I believe you, purely because they're the ones that stand to benefit. They need their meat for the grinder, just like the fuckin' war."

"Yeah, you got that right."

They were both silent as they stood outside, leaned up against the wall. Marquez watched the still trees, still feeling unease in the air. Waters pondered about what he would do if they got off of Petty Island. He wondered if it would just be the same nightmarish totalitarian landscape he came from, or if he would even be able to continue spreading his message. After all, they knew who he and Feig were and knew that they'd be watched even if they went home. They'd just face another execution sentence anyway, if there isn't one awaiting them already, regardless of the outcome of their new mission.

"Fuck it. Let's go see Feig," Waters broke the silence.

"Yeah, we'll just sneak on into the medical wing," Marquez laughed.

Waters stared at him for a few seconds with a blank face as the cigarette hung from his slightly agape mouth, which then turned into a menacing smirk.

"Come on man, there's no way, they'll catch us!"

"What are they going to do? Take us prisoner? Kill us? They already did one of those and I wouldn't hold your breath that the other isn't down the road. Let's just fuckin' do it."

"Alright, alright. Twist my arm. Let's go grab Miller first."

"Alright, sounds good..." Waters paused for a moment, and exclaimed "Shit, where's the gym?" Marquez began laughing, which spread to Waters quickly. "I'm a cantankerous old fuck, why the hell would I be going to the gym!?" Waters said in between bursts of laughter.

"It's a little-ways between here and Schuck's office, come on," Marquez shook his head with a smile on his face. In the back of his mind, he felt an overwhelming sense of dread. Waters' words resonated with him, and the fact that they probably won't be leaving the island alive echoed in the back of his mind as they took off towards the fitness center.

***

For the first time in ages since his arrival at the med bay, his eyelids began to open. The piercing fluorescent lights burned his retinas, which caused him to jerk his head away instinctually. He was finally able to scream. The swift movement of his head agitated the fresh sutures that ran down his chest vertically and in four horizontal lines.

"FUCK!" Feig screamed at the top of his lungs, which he drug out for many seconds. Despite the pain, he felt relieved at being able to move, see, and speak once again. His head was foggy from the anesthetics, and he learned his lesson from jerking his head and carefully scanned the room around him, trying to make out figures and locations as best he could. He first noticed the equipment he was hooked up to, which looked more like engineering diagnostics tools than biological. The robotic surgical arms loomed stiffly over him, pointing drills and blades at him, but with no one to operate them, they were, at the time, innocuous.

It was difficult for him to pick out the sound over the various beeps and hums of the equipment and computers around the room. Countless displays in the nerds' corner, just as he suspected, showed a bunch of graphs and metrics, comparisons and averages, all based around information he unwillingly gathered for them. He picked up the sound of footsteps over the cacophony of the room, and moments later the door opened.

"Mister Feig, I'm glad to see you're up and about. Try not to move too much though, your sutures are still fairly fresh and the sedatives will still linger for a few minutes. You're more than likely experiencing a bit of a head fog right now, but it'll pass once the sedatives wear off. Here, I bought you some water and some actual food."

"Schuck? What are you doing here?"

"Don't worry about that for now, go ahead and eat. Nutrient drips only keep you going during surgery and sedation, you need something real to get your strength back."

Feig didn't respond. He looked down at his plate of food, and despite the fact that it wasn't particularly appetizing, he became voracious and began eating as quickly as he could, chasing each bite with a large gulp of water. After a few minutes, the entire tray was gone, and his stomach hurt from eating so fast, but the satisfaction of finally having food in his stomach was overwhelming.

Schuck sat over in the nerds' corner looking over some nondescript paperwork, occasionally eyeing the charts and graphs.

"So... what are you here for?" Feig said, finally feeling some clarity.

"How are you feeling?" Schuck responded coldly.

"Starting to feel a semblance of normality, I guess," Feig responded. He was annoyed that Schuck didn't answer his question, but he didn't quite have the energy to protest.

"I apologize, I didn't mean to ignore your question, I just want to make sure you're in the right state of mind before we begin. I'm here to do our post combat analysis."

"Didn't the doctors do that already?"

"They performed a *physiological* analysis, yes, but I'm here to do a *psychological* analysis."

"Damn, you're a psychotherapist too? How many hats do you wear, Schuck?"

Schuck bore a rare smirk, "Many, as you've clearly noticed. Before we start, I just need to ask you a few straight forward questions. These serve no purpose in the evaluation, they're just to make sure you're certain who you are and where you are, et cetera, et cetera."

Feig didn't respond.

"What is your full name?"

"Andrew Feig."

"What is your date of birth?"

"September 29th, 2111"

"How old are you?"

"Thirty-four years."

"Where are you currently?"

"I'm in a medical lab operating room in a facility on Petty Island that's housing a Chinese genetic project that ripped my chest open."

Schuck smirked once again. "Well that answers the next question. The good news is, you don't seem to have any obvious psychological trauma at the surface level, but now we're going to go a bit deeper. Feel free to lay back if it makes you more comfortable."

"No thanks, I'll sit up. I've done enough laying around lately," Feig said while averting his eyes.

"Understandable. I'm going to show you a series of pictures, inkblots to be precise, and I want you to tell me what you see."

"Holtzman or Rorschach? And weren't those abandoned, like, eighty years ago? The psych community moved on to more modern methods and technology."

"I'm impressed, you seem to know your stuff. To answer your first question, we'll be using the Rorschach test, the Holtzman inkblots were more for personality profiles. As for the other, while majority of the psychological community may not see worth in them, I have, at least anecdotally, determined them to be useful in scenarios such as this."

"And what scenario is this, exactly?"

"Post combat trauma. Historically, getting soldiers to speak about what they've seen or done has been extremely difficult. It wasn't until the advent of the 2100's when methylenedioxymethamphetamine exited clinical studies and went into full usage that we were able to get clear answers."

"You're going to dose me on molly? Why not just look at the footage? You record it all, don't you?"

"Combat footage tells us a *what, when,* and *where,* but not a *why* or *how.* As for the medication, not initially. This is where the value for the inkblots comes into play. By gauging your responses before and after medication, I'll be able to look for inconsistencies between the two and read between the lines, for lack of a better phrase."

"Doesn't telling me all of this affect the test? I could lie or alter things."

"You could, and in some instances, I expect you to. I devised this test for precisely this purpose, so respond however you wish. I would appreciate honesty, but even if you choose to lie, I'll still be able to put a picture together. Shall we begin?"

Feig let out a short sigh and rubbed his brow, groaning slightly at the pain that moving his arm created in his chest.

Schuck waved his hand over an interface on a portable tablet he had resting on his lap. A display at the end of the surgical chair, usually used for surgical cameras and biological displays, displayed an inkblot image.

"What do you see here?"

Feig looked at the image intently. Images of the Manticore charging at him, its claws extended and mouth agape, flashed in his mind.

"A dog."

"Very good. How about this one?" Schuck waved his hand again and the ink on the display morphed and convulsed into a new image.

Feig wiped the sweat that was beading on his forehead with the back of his arm. Another shot of pain ran through the stitches in his chest. His mind flashed images of the sub levels, of himself looking at his own body, unable to move, shortly before being dragged onto the elevator.

"Some wild flowers, I think?"

"Good, and this one?" Schuck waved his hand once more and the picture danced into the form of a new one.

He didn't know if it was the lousy food, or coming down off of the sedative, but he began to feel nauseous. He saw images of Marquez in the sub level, talking to the Manticore like a person. Something wasn't right.

"A boy and a girl. Holding hands, maybe?"

"Very interesting. My apologies, mister Feig, it looks like you may be suffering some adverse effects from the sedatives, we have some more medication here if you'd like."

"No, no. I'll just ride it out. I think I need to lay down for a bit anyway."

"Very well, I'll be back in a few hours to resume to test. If you need anything, use the interface on the chair to call a nurse, they'll get you food or drink as you need it," Schuck said while using his tablet to interact with the surgical chair. The sharp ends of the surgical arms became shielded and began to sterilize.

"I wasn't going to off myself, Schuck," Feig said weakly.

"I didn't think you were, mister Feig. Just standard procedure. One that one of our medical staff clearly forgot to follow."

Schuck left the room and closed the door gently behind him. Feig felt exhausted and laid down in the surgical chair. He slowly raised his arm to cover his eyes to avoid agitating his stitches. He couldn't shake the fear he felt as images of the Manticore continued to cloud his mind. He was thankful for the exhaustion to force him to sleep.

***

Miller was covered in sweat, using a bench to perform butterfly press while laying down. When he heard the door open, he sat up, resting the weights on his thighs.

"What's up guys? Decided to join me in some self-punishment? Might as well make a good-looking corpse, you know what I mean?" Miller said with a smile.

"We're going to go check on Feig," Waters responded.

"I thought they weren't letting anyone in yet? Some bullshit spiel about optimal recovery times."

"They're not, but we're going anyway," Marquez added.

"What are you nuts? They'll fucking kill us!"

"Yeah that's what I said too, but Waters made a pretty compelling argument."

"And what was that?"

"Man, no wonder you guys are buddies. Like I told Joey, chances are they're going to kill us anyway once we're done dealing with the Manticore, so what are they going to do? Kill their crack team before they can do what they're being forced to do? No. We can go see Feig and they can bitch us out, but ultimately they need us, so fuck it."

Miller wiped himself down with a towel and stared at the floor for a few moments. "Well, shit. When you put it like that... Let me get a shower and get changed real quick. Poor guy got ripped open, I doubt the first thing he wants to see is a gross, sweaty wop."

"Make it quick, we're going to grab a quick smoke, come out when you're done and we'll figure out how we're going to get in there," Waters said with urgency.

"Two minutes, promise!" Miller said, as he ran off to the showers.

Marquez and Waters went outside to have another quick smoke. Marquez looked at Waters, smirked, and shook his head. He didn't have to say it out loud, but Waters knew basically what he was conveying. *This is fucking crazy and I can't believe we're doing it.*

Miller came out of the door with his hair still wet, but freshly dressed and energetic.

"Alright so what's the deal? How are we going to do this?" Miller said excitedly.

"I don't want to talk about it here, too many eyes and ears. Let's do a sweep of the island. You know, research purposes," Waters said with obvious guile in his voice.

"I gotcha, I gotcha," Miller said with a smile.

They went to the armory and geared up, then quickly approached the main gate.

"I don't have you guys doing a sortie today, what's with the getups?" the guard asked snarkily.

"Come on man, what the fuck else are we supposed to do? Can't sit in the cafeteria jerking off all day."

"I have to run it through the commander, let me call it in."

Marquez, Waters, and Miller looked at each other, and back at the guard.

"Commander, the prisoners are trying to take a walk on the island, should I open the gate?"

Commander Wilkins opened up the comms channel to the prisoners, "What's the matter gentlemen, getting antsy?"

"A little bit, but we just figured with Feig holed up in medical, we could try to plot out some better entrance and escape routes. Stretch our legs a little in the process," Marquez responded.

"I don't see the harm. Open the gate for them. Gentlemen, you know the curfew. Gate closes before sundown, be back before then, or you're camping."

"Yeah, yeah, we know the drill," Marquez retorted.

The guard made a smug smile at the group and hit the switch to open the pressurized gate, and the three made their way towards the center of the island.

"Okay, so what's the deal?" Miller said prematurely. Waters slapped him on the back of the helmet with a loud metallic thud.

"What the fuck was that for?!" Miller exclaimed.

Waters then slapped Marquez on the back of the helmet, and finally, his own helmet.

"It's amazing how an institution so powerful can be so fucking stupid. We used to put magnets by the transceiver in the helmet back when we were enlisted. It completely blocks signals both incoming and outgoing. Any time we wanted to talk shit on superiors or if someone was selling some good stuff, we'd just slap a neodymium magnet on it and do business."

"Shit, me and Marquez never heard about that!"

"That's because you weren't with the nerds in the engineering regiment. Feig was always finding ways around protocols and limiters. Do you still wonder why we don't think these same people should be telling us how to live?"

"Every day we're stuck here I understand you two more and more," Miller said with a laugh.

"Wait, where the fuck did you get magnets?" Miller interjected.

"They had some in the cafeteria." Waters responded.

"Jesus Christ, seriously?" Marquez was dumbfounded.

"Seriously. So, we want to sneak into the med bay, but your next question is going to be 'how?' Luckily, in another glaring example of the government's ineptitude, when they gave us the schematics for our first dip into the sub levels, it included the whole damn island."

"You're shitting me!" Marquez said in disbelief.

"I wish I was, but Christ if they don't make it too easy for us. Pull up the med bay on your HUDs."

Miller and Marquez manipulated some buttons on the side of their helmets and were shocked to see a layout of the building they planned on sneaking into.

"So, if you look here at the main view, there are three main points of entry. The main entrance, which also happens to be the emergency doors, will never be locked in case they need to haul a body in, like they did with Feig. The catch of course is that it's most likely to be the most guarded. That, and if you zoom in a little, you can see it's almost entirely covered by camera views. Probably not our best option. However," Waters adjusted the layout view to the side of the medical building, "on the eastern side of the building, towards the wall, there's a roll up door here that's marked 'receiving' as well as 'refuse'. This is most likely where they bring in supplies, large machines, as well as where they take the trash out. Considering no one wants to stand around medical waste all day, it's least likely to be guarded, and has minimal camera coverage. The catch here is that there's a turret directly nearby, so we have to find a way to make sure the guard operating it doesn't see us. The third, and my least favorite option, is through the sub level."

"Whoa, whoa, what? I thought they annexed it off?" Miller interjected.

"They did, but if you zoom in on the western side of the building, it looks like there's an access shaft that hooks up to the maintenance tunnels and brings you into the power hub of the medical bay. Probably for easy access between the two for the maintenance guys before shit went down and they blocked it off. That said, the room we'd need to get to in the sub level is blocked by rubble, which is why we didn't see it when we were down there before. We'd have to spend some time moving it out of the way, but it would take us there. My issue with this one, outside of the obvious, is that there's no guarantee they didn't weld the hatch shut in the medical bay, which I'm going to say they probably did."

"Why didn't you just cut the shit and say we're using the receiving entrance?" Marquez said.

"Habit, I guess. I like people to know all of their options before we dive into the shit," Waters replied.

"Okay so we know where we're going in, but what do we do once we get in there?" Miller asked.

"This is where it gets a little murky. I don't know for sure where they're keeping him, but based on the schematic, I'd say closer to the surgical ward or the research ward."

"That makes sense. What kind of patrols are we expecting?" Marquez said with growing interest.

"That I'm not sure of, but from what I can tell, most of the patrols are manning the walls and primary entrance points. Inside the building, I don't know if they entirely give a shit. I mean, think about it, nobody gets on this island that they don't want here, they're probably not planning for someone that's already here to try to break into one of the buildings."

"Shit, this might be a cakewalk," Miller said with surprise.

"Exactly. So, our only obstacle is going to be the guards on the wall, but if we just hug the sides, I honestly think we can walk right the fuck in there."

Marquez began to laugh, "Jesus Christ. You know, in all those old spy movies, they make getting in or out of these buildings this whole dramatic song and dance, but all it really takes is three bored assholes with too much time on their hands."

Miller and Waters began to laugh as well. Waters took the magnets off of their helmets one by one, and began speaking relevant nonsense to ease suspicion.

"So, if we run into a similar scenario, we won't have to depend on the elevator next time, we can secure access to the hatch and block it off if need be."

"Copy that," Marquez responded.

The sun was beginning to set, and the three prisoners began making their way back to the main gate to prepare for their infiltration.

***

Dreams of the Manticore plagued him as he slept, but they didn't plague him for much longer. The sound of the door handle woke him up. Feig shot out of bed, and immediately groaned in pain from the sudden movement. His stitches felt worse as the sedatives had all worn off.

"Good evening, mister Feig. I'm sorry if I alarmed you. How are you feeling?" Schuck said.

Feig didn't respond. He was still in a half-asleep haze, trying to get his bearings.

"I wanted to get around to the second half of the tests. Are you feeling better? Earlier this afternoon you seemed a bit uncomfortable."

"Yeah, no, I'm fine, just trying to wake up a bit. Shit these stitches hurt," Feig replied sleepily.

"The damage to your tissue was quite extensive, but between the fiber mesh and structural support the surgeons put in, structurally you might even be better than you were before. The pain should subside much faster as well. Luckily for you, the medicine you'll be taking for the next part of the test will also help you with that, albeit temporarily."

"Yeah, you're going to jack me up on molly, right?"

"The street name was indeed "molly," but yes, I'm going to be giving you a metered dose of methylenedioxymethamphetamine. I'm going to start you at two tenths of a gram, and after thirty minutes, four tenths of a gram. After another thirty minutes, I'll give you a final four tenths for a full gram. Any more than that is superfluous, and any less won't be effective enough. If you would please, sit up in the chair so I can hook it up to your cannula."

Feig hesitated, but slowly sat himself up.

"Some apprehension is to be expected, but you are indeed in the medical bay, we'll be watching your vitals closely to ensure that no harm comes of you, and you shouldn't experience any adverse side effects in regards to your wound healing. We'll give you a serotonin supplement for the next few days so that your chemicals don't become imbalanced."

"Whatever you say, Schuck. You know, we used to pay a pretty penny for this on the street."

Schuck scoffed, "If only you knew how important of a medicinal purpose this had and why it must only be used as such."

Schuck injected the metered dose while Feig continued to speak, "So you really buy that? That banning it did anything? Marijuana was legal for sixty years without any real issue, but once you guys swept in to save the day, you banned it all for 'the greater good.' What has it gotten you? More densely populated prisons? A larger tax burden?"

"You surprise me, mister Feig. I don't think the drug works that fast, and yet you've spoken more here than I think I've heard during your entire stay!" Schuck said with surprise in his voice.

"I know... I know I'm shy, but I just can't stand seeing otherwise intelligent people spouting off mindless rhetoric. Then again, you went through the state schools and got high placement in the military, so I can't blame you for not biting the hand that feeds you."

For once, Schuck didn't respond. Instead, he focused on watching Feig's vitals on his tablet, checking the time. A long period of silence went by, and Feig began to feel the effects of the drug.

"My hands just got cold. It's like it's creeping up my arm," Feig said in a slightly slowed voice.

"That is correct. That feeling will wash over you completely in a few minutes. I'm going to administer the second dosage, and then just another short wait for the final dose and we can begin. Your heart rate has increased as expected, and it's still within viable ranges, as is your body temperature. You will probably begin to sweat in a few minutes, I have plenty of water and a fan if you begin to feel uncomfortable."

"I feel... just a little fucked up. Am I speaking in slow motion? I feel like I'm speaking in slow motion," Feig said, very much in what would have been perceived by an outside party as slow motion.

"Time may dilate a little for you, so the wait until the next dosage might seem longer for you than it will for me," Schuck responded.

As time went on, Feig began rubbing his hands and legs on things around him, with Schuck intervening to make sure he didn't hurt himself or accidentally remove the cannula in his arm. He began to laugh and move in odd ways.

"Can I have a cigarette, Schuck? I would reeeeeeally like a cigarette. Oh my god, I feel incredible. You need to try this, Schuck," Feig said with his eyes practically rolling around his head. Schuck, without a word, pulled out an ornate case from his breast pocket and opened it up, revealing long, slender cigarettes that were in a dark brown paper. He handed one to Feig and lit it for him.

"Hooooooooooly fuck, Chuck," Feig began to laugh, "holy fuck Chuck, get it? You know, you may be a fucking hard ass, but you're alright sometimes. I mean, you're gonna kill us all, but you're alright sometimes. Ffffffffffffffuck man, this is unreeeeeeeal, it's like a wave washing over me."

Schuck lit himself a cigarette and gently placed the case back in his breast pocket. "The effects are indeed well documented, mister Feig. I'm going to administer the final dose and we will continue the test, is that okay?"

"Chuck this is increeeeeeeeeeeeedible!" Feig writhed in place, rubbing his hands and legs around in place, while Schuck attempted to steady Feig's arm to inject the final dosage.

"I'm sorry Chuck, I'm getting in the way, aren't I? Everything just feels so amazing, I thought all those kids back in the day were full of shit with their stuffed animal toys but hoooooooooly fuuuuuuuuuuuuuck."

"Mister Feig, I'm going to show you some images, are you ready?"

"Yeah man, go right ahead, hoooooooooooly shit."

Schuck waved his hand over the interface, and an image appeared on the display at the end of the surgical chair. It was the same first image he was shown before.

"Please, let me know what you see here."

Feig's intense euphoria washed over his entire body. Every sensation he felt was amplified a hundred-fold. His brow was covered in sweat, but he didn't mind. He took a drag of the dark cigarette and looked at the ink blot as best he could, with his head swaying back and forth in bliss.

"It's the fucking Manticore, Chuck. It's the manticore. Goooooood damn it this feels so good."

"Very good. How about this next picture?" Schuck once again waved his hand over the interface, and the image swirled and settled into a new image. This time, it was the second picture he saw earlier.

Feig began to laugh wildly, "That's me! That's me after I got attacked. See here? There's like, my legs, and my right arm was kind of like, across my chest there. See it?" Feig was unable to articulate a lie, and he felt no desire to. He hated Schuck for being an agent of the state, he hated everything he represented, but he just wanted to share his thoughts and feelings truthfully, so that he knew he shared them with someone before he died.

"Interesting, how about this final picture?"

The shapes waltzed once again, forming the final picture he had seen earlier that day. Feig tried to look at it, but an immeasurably intense wave of pleasure and joy overcame him at that moment.

"Fuuuuuuuuuuuuuuuuuuck meeeee this feels amazing. What if life was always like this? What if you were like this? You wouldn't be torturing girls on an island, that's for sure."

"I'm sorry, mister Feig? Could you please elaborate."

"The girl, Chuck. The girl you have here. That last picture, it looks like Joey talking to the girl after she carved me up."

Schuck didn't say a word. He sat and stared for a minute while Feig writhed in joy.

"Make sure to drink your water, mister Feig. The nurses are monitoring your vitals, and if you need anything, feel free to call them. You have anywhere between eight and twelve hours until you're back to normal, so enjoy yourself, I suppose."

Schuck left the room abruptly and slammed the door on his way out. Feig couldn't work out whether it was intentional or not, but he couldn't care any less as he continued to play around with everything around him and roll around in the surgical chair.

***

The night had come, and the crushing silence had taken over the island. No crickets, no birds, just a barely audible splashing of water on the banks of the island in the distance. Marquez, Miller, and Waters were in the mess hall, eating a late dinner after spending the afternoon meandering the island to plan their infiltration of the med bay to check up on their injured friend.

"I don't know about you guys, but I'm not really quite tired yet. Wanna maybe take a walk? Grab a smoke?" Waters said, breaking the silence.

"Sounds good to me. Miller?"

"Sure, why not? We haven't gotten any word about our next dip anyway, and I don't think I'm getting to sleep any time soon."

The three walked out of the cafeteria, and Waters distributed cigarettes to everyone. They began walking along the wall, chit-chatting about how bad the food was and how low they are on the scotch that the commander gave them. A few guards patrolling the wall passed by them and didn't pay any notice to them. Another guard shined his flashlight at the group. Waters waved and the guard returned to his patrol.

"I fuckin' told you guys. These guards have it so damn easy here they're apathetic, and apathy leads to holes in security," Waters whispered.

"Maybe one of us should peel off for a bit to make it look like we're not up to something," Marquez whispered back.

"That's not a bad idea. It would make sense for you two to stick together, since you're boys and what not. We'll just stand here and have a nice conversation for the cameras, I'll wave and you guys can go around. We'll meet up a little-ways down the wall, sound good?"

"Sounds good to me. Try not to draw too much attention and we'll do the same. See you in a few minutes."

Waters waved at the pair, and they went their separate ways.

Marquez and Miller split off down a well-lit path past a few guards. They overheard them talking about how boring it is having to keep watch over entrances and how they much prefer the wall because they get to see civilization for a bit. Miller and Marquez made fun of them while they walked around slowly, taking small drags off of their cigarettes which were about halfway finished.

Waters stuck to the wall, with one hand in his pocket and the other holding the cigarette. The stark silence was broken by a guard on the wall hollering down at him.

"Hey, prisoner! Why aren't you in your bunk?"

"Couldn't sleep, man, wanted to take a quick stroll and have a smoke, is that alright?"

"You're not supposed to be out past curfew."

"If the thing attacks, I'm unarmed anyway. You're the one on the wall with the turrets, are you really worried about me?"

The guard paused for a moment, "Just make it quick, alright?"

"I won't be out much longer, just going to go until I'm done my smoke and then head back to the bunks. Won't be long, I promise."

The guard scoffed and continued his patrol along the wall. After many minutes went by, Waters heard the crunching of grass and leaves coming from the right of him. The dim orange in the distance let him know that it was Marquez and Miller, but he wanted to be sure and snuffed out his cigarette and hid along the wall.

"It's us, man. You ready?" Marquez whispered.

Waters let out a hushed sigh of relief, "Yeah, let's go. It shouldn't be too far. Hug the wall and tread lightly."

The three, now regrouped, proceeded through the ever-darker woods, lit only dimly by ambient light from the spotlights along the wall occasionally passing by. They stepped in such a way that reduced the crunch of the leaves underneath their feet to a whisper, which in any other context would be a very strange gait. Through the trees, their eyes finally met the medical building, which was bleeding fluorescent light onto the surrounding forest, giving it an eerie glow.

"You ready fellas?" Waters uttered, barely exhaling.

Marquez and Miller nodded, and the group resumed their silent steps towards the eastern side of the building. Waters threw his hand up, signaling the other two to stop. Shortly after, he peeked his head around the corner of the building to look for any signs of patrols. He waved his hand and they began moving towards a single light emitted from a fixture above a roll up loading door a few feet off of the ground.

"So how are we getting in?" Marquez asked.

"Don't know yet, but I'm betting on them not locking the loading door," Waters responded.

"And if it is?"

"We try a window, or another entrance."

Marquez was beginning to have second thoughts about their daring infiltration, but knew he was already in too deep, and truthfully, he genuinely wanted to see if Feig was okay.

Waters looked around hectically before digging his hands underneath the loading door. He strained with a light grunt as the door made a shrill creak and ultimately didn't move anywhere.

"Shit," Waters said without showing any emotion on his face.

"I'll try a window," Marquez said after seeing the defeat in Waters' eyes.

Marquez and Waters both began prying at the windows within their reach. They cursed under their breath when they realized each one was locked. Minutes of time bumping windows, looking for one unlocked, when finally, they looked over and saw a large beam of light emitting from the side of the building. Standing directly in the light, perfectly illuminated, was Miller, who found a regular personnel door. He proceeded to twist the knob and open it.

"You're fuckin' kidding me," Waters stated, followed by a short, sharp sigh.

Waters and Marquez went over to the door and met up with Miller who had a sarcastically proud grin across his face, to which Waters gave an unimpressed grimace as he passed him on his way into the building.

The brightly lit hallways temporarily blinded them, causing them to squint as they checked the two hallways for nurses, doctors, and guards. The building felt empty, which was disconcerting at first, but relieving after Waters blurted out, "Of course it's empty, how many people could be on this island? A hundred, tops?"

Marquez and Miller looked at each other with a shrug, and the group began looking for signs to follow to find the surgical unit. Miller spotted one and gestured to the other two to follow him. Waters watched the group's back, while Marquez did his best to check into side rooms without being obvious. The group hunched down low and hugged the walls to stay out of potential eyesight.

Miller heard the sounds of machines beeping and a low moan coming from around the next corner they were approaching. He immediately picked up the pace, with Marquez and Waters to follow. Miller and Marquez positioned themselves on either side of the door and watched either direction to make sure no one was coming while Waters crept his face up to the window in the door. He peered in and saw Feig writhing in his surgical bed and immediately flung the door open.

"Phiiiiiiiiiil! Filibuster... Filipino. Felipe. You brought the guys too! Guys - you *have* to see if Chuck will give you some of this, hooooooooly shit," Feig said. He dragged out his letters and writhed in place as the waves of euphoria washed over him.

"Are... are you rolling balls right now?" Waters asked with a face blanketed in confusion.

"Dude I'm not even rolling, I'm on another fucking plaaaaaanet right now."

Marquez and Miller stifled laughter into their forearms. Waters' confusion began to melt away into a smile, followed by laughter.

"Jesus Christ, here we thought they were torturing you and they're giving you all the good shit while

126

we're pulling our dicks in the cafeteria!" Waters exclaimed.

Miller prudently shut the door gently, while still trying not to laugh.

"Damn, Feig! We had to run spec ops to get in here to see how you were doing, had I known they were drugging you up I might have leapt in front of that thing to get a piece of the action," Marquez added, still laughing.

"No, yeah I'm fiiiiiine man. After the stupid inkblot test, well, the first one, Chuck came in to do another but gave me a bunch of molly first. What a guy, I tell you," Feig responded with his eyelids drooping. He rubbed his hands along the guard rails of the surgical bed.

"Why did he give you an inkblot test? That's like that shit where they try to pry into your mind with abstract pictures and shit, right?" Waters asked.

"Yeeeeah, he wanted me to tell him about the girl."

Marquez's face turned sallow, and his heart sank into his stomach. *He saw her too*, Marquez thought, *He fucking saw her too. How? He must have seen her as she was crawling into the room I found her in. Before she changed back...*

Waters and Miller looked at each other puzzled, but brushed off the comment, writing it off as the drugs talking.

"Feig, guys, I wanted to-" Marquez began to speak, but was cut off by the handle of the door turning.

The three reactively leapt away from the door and began to grab the nearest items they could find to use as weapons. The door opened slightly and a familiar face peeked in.

"Good evening gentlemen. I imagine you're here to check on mister Feig?"

"CHUCK?!" Waters yelled.

"I'm right here, mister Waters. Would you all mind putting down the expensive medical equipment you're all holding?"

They each placed down the various medical paraphernalia they had grabbed instinctively, and Schuck gently opened the door completely and entered the room, closing the door behind him.

"You're probably wondering why I've administered a federally banned substance to your fellow soldier. I was simply-"

"Claaaaaaaassic government hypocrisy, Chuck. Banned for us, okay for you, right?" Feig said while rolling his head around his shoulders and laughing.

"I was simply utilizing a technique, completely scientific in nature mind you, for comparing two sets of data to get some more... honest answers about what you all experienced in the sub levels."

"Shit, man, you could have told us there'd be a reward for getting hacked up," Marquez said with a chuckle. Schuck didn't break a smile.

"Mister Marquez, what we're doing here is of an extremely important nature, as I'm sure you understand by now, and my use of otherwise illicit substances was necessary, and it was done in a controlled environment."

"Wait wait wait wait," Waters interjected, "You're not going to call the guards or throw us in a cell?"

"Well, as you stated yourself upon arrival to the Island, mister Waters, you're technically already in one, are you not? Anyway, it's not as if you planned to break him out of here. Taking him away from medical attention would be counterintuitive, don't you think?"

Waters grunted.

"Anyway, gentlemen, mister Feig is slated to make a full recovery. He has been treated with the best methods and equipment that the DRA has at its disposal, and you'll be ready to deploy in a few weeks. He has reacted beautifully to the synthetic stem cell treatment we've applied to the wound, and it's healing at an accelerated rate. It should be healed within a few days, but he'll need some extra recovery time to ensure he's back up to his optimal performance. You'll be free to roam the island for some fresh air once again, and when you're ready, we'll call you for preparation. Feel free to stay with him as long as you wish, I'll radio the guards and let them know that you're cleared to be out past curfew for this evening."

Waters scoffed, while Marquez gave a slight nod to Schuck.

"Farewell, gentlemen," Schuck then left the room, gently closing the door behind him.

The group spent hours into the night telling stories about their daring infiltration and poking fun at Feig for being comically high. Once the drug wore off and the sun began to peek from behind the horizon, Feig expressed his exhaustion, and the three each gave him their well wishes and left the medical building. As they left, the medical staff arriving for their shifts gave them confused, and others, angry looks as they passed by, while the group simply laughed and ran down the halls like kids being let out of school early. When they got back to their bunks, they plopped down heavily into them and slept like stones, only after a minute or so of giggling sleepily at the events that had unfolded.

**

"The most urgent necessity is, not that the State should teach, but that it should allow education. All monopolies are detestable, but the worst of all is the monopoly of education."
— Frédéric Bastiat

Chapter 6 - Fear of The Dark

In his dream, Marquez saw the girl again. She looked terrified and angry all at the same time.

"Don't do that, please don't fucking do that!" he screamed at her, but it was as if his voice was miles away.

Her eyes locked with his, and in an instant, she had transformed into the Manticore, a hulking mound of flesh, and clawed him across the torso. He looked down to see familiar organs and blood pouring out of the hole in his gut. When he looked up, the girl was covering her mouth, weeping, as tears and blood streamed gently down her cheek.

Marquez awoke and checked the time.

"Shit," he said in a muffled whisper, "only twelve oh six?"

He rubbed his cold hand across his brow and tugged the blanket back up and over his shoulders. As he turned over to try to go back to sleep, he couldn't shake the imagery of the girl standing over him in his dream. Bawling and afraid, yet covered in his blood. Her long, black hair twisted and curled gracefully over her shoulders. It looked as if it were underwater in the way it moved. Slowly, and relative to her movements it danced, and bounced along with her trembling shoulders. She wept at him as he bled. Her unsullied hand pulled away from her quivering lips and extended towards him, as if to offer assistance or an apology. He reached his right hand out to hers. The dream always ended there.

I have to tell them, he thought, still not believing himself, *I have to tell them she's not a monster. Shit.*

Marquez didn't sleep as well as the other prisoners, but he was extremely alert come breakfast time.

"What, did you beat Waters to the coffee pot this morning?" Miller quipped.

"No, man. Just had a hell of a night, that's all," Marquez responded.

Waters plopped down across from Marquez and Miller, next to Feig as always. His food tray made a loud crack as it landed on the table, and a bit of his hash browns went flying off of it.

"You know it's only a matter of time now, right boys?" Waters said rhetorically. "Chuck said it'd be a couple of weeks and then they'd be throwing us back into the shit. I was convinced they were going to change their minds and execute us anyway after last week's infiltration fiasco, but I'm betting we've got less than seven days to our next trip to the fucking graveyard."

"Listen, guys, about that," Marquez slapped the back of his own head a few times with his left hand, "I was hoping we could do a little patrolling, you know? Stay fresh and all."

The group looked around at each other for a bit and knew what he was getting at.

"Sounds good to me. Next time we see that fuckin' thing, I want to be prepared," Waters said, making sure to play the part.

"For sure, I don't want Feig to have to spend another week rolling balls!" Miller added with a laugh.

Feig didn't say anything, but he smirked and nodded.

They finished their breakfast and turned in their trays as fast as they could to chase the meal down with a cigarette. Feig relented to the offer, and the four smoked vigorously and anxiously on their way to the armory. The guards and clerks no longer paid them much mind, as they knew that the prisoners were clear to patrol the island as they chose.

The four geared up and made their way to the gate. The gate guard gave them his trademark sarcastic grin. The hydraulics let out their familiar hiss as the gate opened and allowed the prisoners passage from one cage into the other. No one said a word as they crunched the grass with every step towards the middle of the island. Waters began slapping magnets onto everyone's helmets. He made sure to place them directly on top of the communications transceiver.

"Alright Joey, so what's the word?" Waters didn't skip a beat.

"Okay, so look... this is going to sound fucking crazy, I ju-..." Marquez struggled to get the words out. He knew how it would sound to them, but he knew it was true.

"Crazier than a military bio-engineering experiment hidden on a piece of shit island between Camden and Philly? Come on man!" Waters joked. Miller chuckled.

"You're probably not going to believe me, but yeah crazier than that. That... thing isn't just a fucking monster. It's a girl."

The group fell silent for a minute. Feig averted his eyes and began to grow pale.

"How do you figure it's female? Schuck's diagrams didn't exactly go over the intricacies of its genitalia," Waters finally broke the silence.

"Her, Phil. Her geni-... it's a girl, alright? Like a human girl. After it tore open Feig, you were busy calling for a medic, remember? I saw a human leg go into one of the nearby rooms. When I went in there, there was a girl. She was curled up in the corner, naked. Crying and shaking. I tried to help her and then she..."

"You've gotta be fuckin' kidding me!" Waters interjected.

"She changed into the thing and took off! I told you it sounds fucking crazy, I wouldn't believe it myself if I didn't see her with my own two fucking eyes, Phil! Feig, I know you saw it. That's what Schuck was doing with the drugs, right? You said it yourself, he was asking you about the girl, you saw her!"

"Feig was fucked up on a gram of molly, he probably *imagined* a girl for Christ's sake!" Waters said loudly.

"I saw her, Phil. After she attacked me, I saw her crawl into that room..." Feig said sheepishly.

"There's no way dude, no WAY!" Miller said, "Look guys, we've been stuck at this place for how long now? We were in close quarters combat, Feig got nearly killed, and tensions were high. Your minds are playing tricks on you!"

"Miller's right, Joey, I mean come on, a fucking girl that can shapeshift into a killing machine? Did you steal some of the drugs from the surgical bay?" Waters said as Miller was finishing his sentence.

"Listen, we all saw some horrible shit during the war, and we all saw real fucking combat. That firefight was horrible combat, but there's no way it would cause the two of us to spontaneously hallucinate. I told you it would be crazy, but I'm not making shit up, and I didn't just imagine it either!"

"Look, I know the powers that be are capable of some heinous shit. I got sentenced to death for telling people about it for Christ's sake, but are you really suggesti-"

"If it is a girl and you fucking kill her when they send us down there in a week, would you be able to live with yourself?" Marquez said angrily.

The prisoners fell silent once again. Minutes went by like blinks of an eye. Miller kicked twigs and stones around. Feig sat on the ground with his arms draped over his knees, staring pensively into the distance. Waters paced back and forth, trying to process the implications of what Marquez said.

Fuck. If it's a girl, there's a good chance she's not here by choice, and if we killed her and she isn't, then we're just as bad as the bastards that brought her here in the first place, Waters' mind raced, *Shit. SHIT.*

"SHIT! Alright, so say it is a girl, what do we do?" Waters yelled to Marquez.

"I want to try to talk to her again. When we were down there, I put my hand out and told her we were there to help. At that point we had already shot at her and Feig got injured, so I'm not entirely surprised if she thought I was lying, but I think we can talk to her."

"And then what? She talks, you two fall in love, we have a fucking campfire singalong and they let us go?"

"I don't know! I don't know yet, we'll figure it out from there. Let's just... let's just split up and finish our patrol. Take the magnets off once we get a good distance away from each other and check in to play the part. For now, we wait until they tell us we're going back underground."

***

A few tense, quiet days passed and the day the prisoners were waiting for was finally upon them. The distinctive klaxon blared in their ears, and they all calmly made their way to the armory to gear up. No one spoke, and they barely made eye contact as they armed themselves with various weapons of their choice. They made sure to stock up on extra magazines of the experimental ammunition and explosives. Their heavy, metallic marching rang out on the catwalks as they trudged to strategic operations, and still, no one spoke. When they arrived, they once again found the door open, waiting for them. They piled in and took their seats.

"Good morning gentlemen. Mister Feig, glad to see you've made a full recovery. May I skip the rest of the formalities and get straight to business?" Schuck stated rhetorically.

The prisoners nodded in agreement.

"Excellent. Now that mister Feig is back up to full combat potential and you've all had some time to clear your heads from your last engagement, we want to send you back in. This time, a little bit more prepared, and a little bit wiser. You're soldiers. You learn from your mistakes. You adapt."

Schuck motioned his hands above the interface to bring up combat data from their last encounter with the Manticore.

"As you can see, we've gathered, collated, and analyzed quite a bit of data from your last trip to the sub level. We were able to find a precise timing for its regenerative abilities. It seems it's faster than we first estimated, it's able to regenerate damaged tissue within thirteen seconds - faster if the wound is less severe. That said, the ammunition did seem to have a slowing effect on this process. When you were able to hit it in key points with the ammunition, the regeneration time was slowed to well over thirty seconds. This is promising because if you can continue that trend, you should be able to stop it long enough for us to contain it."

The prisoners didn't speak or move.

"Is there a problem?" Schuck asked inquisitively.

"No, sir. We've been preparing for this for a few weeks now, save for Feig. We're just taking it all in, you know?" Marquez said nervously.

"Very well. As you can see here," Schuck said as he gestured his hand, "these spots are where the regenerative slowing effect was most pronounced. In between its plates, the flesh seems to be more... 'normal', for lack of a better term, than the rest of it. If you target these spots consistently, I believe you will be successful in subduing it. I've transferred this information as well as some of the extended ballistics data to your heads-up displays. Any questions?"

The prisoners were silent.

"Very well. Proceed to the main gate for deployment by zero seven hundred. The sun will be up and you'll have maximum time in the sub level. Dismissed."

The prisoners didn't nod or speak. They got up from their seats and exited the strategic operations room one by one. They made their way back to the main gate in complete silence. The guard didn't even give them his signature smirk as he opened the gate for them to enter the island's mainland. After a few minutes of walking, they found themselves at the hatch.

"Alright guys, like we practiced," Marquez finally spoke.

The other three prisoners nodded.

The rusty hatch squealed and clanked as they pried it open, revealing the dark, damp passageway to the very same depths where Feig was mauled.

"Hey, you okay?" Waters said, looking over at Feig. Feig nodded diffidently.

"Come on, I'll go first," Waters said to reassure him.

Waters began making his way down the damp ladder, and his armor clanked against each rung. Miller followed shortly after, with Marquez and finally Feig making their own ways down.

The sight was familiar, yet somehow alien. Dark, damp corridors, puddles with overgrowth around them, and the dust lingering in the air highlighted by the beams of light emitted from their helmets.

"How could I forget how much I fuckin' hated this place?" Waters remarked.

"Waters, you want to take rear with Feig? Miller, come on up front. Keep your eyes open, and from now on keep chatter to a minimum, we need to listen for it as much as we need to look for it, alright?" Marquez said.

"You got it, Joey," Miller added.

The musty air filled their noses with a dank, dusty fragrance. The prisoners looked around the corridors to get their bearings. Feig saw his own dried blood on the floor and walls. He knew exactly where they were. Feig jumped at the feeling of a hand on his shoulder. Waters, trying to comfort him, but unintentionally scared him, which caused Feig to break the silence less than gracefully, "Jesus fucking Christ, Phil!"

"Sorry Andy, I know it's gotta be a little fucked up seeing your own blood here..." Waters apologized in a not-so-quiet whisper.

"Shh!" Marquez shushed the two abruptly.

The prisoners proceeded to tread softly and carefully past the doorway to the elevator, their salvation from their last trek into the sub level. The puddles of water and mud gurgled beneath their boots, echoing faintly in the cramped, labyrinthine passageways. A loud thud came from their right.

"Did you hear that?!" Miller whispered anxiously.

"East side, let's move," Marquez whispered back.

The group turned to the east and began making their way down the hallway. They altered their steps to make as little noise as possible, each readied their weapons instinctively. A gasping, guttural sound came from behind them. Waters and Feig turned around and their flashlights illuminated the walls and floor. They saw nothing but dust and puddles as Feig let out a sigh of relief. The sound turned into a piercing screech, as an arc of violet light blitzed past them, which culminated in a loud, thunderous crack.

On the floor in front of Marquez and Miller, a large mound of flesh began bubbling and gyrating as the Manticore began to take form. Its hellish howl stabbed at their ears and disoriented them. Marquez quickly tried to shake it off and began to speak.

"We're not here to hurt you! Please listen to me, I know you're in there!"

The creature shrieked once again and reared up on its haunches, before leaping towards them with an open maw. Marquez put his arm out to keep Miller from firing, raising his own weapon in his other hand vertically. The Manticore stopped in front of them and growled lowly.

"Do you remember me? I saw you in the room around the corner. You didn't look like this, remember? I'm Joey. Joey Marquez."

The creature gazed at them attentively. Moments passed without anyone saying a word.

"What are you doing? Shoot it!" Schuck bellowed over their communicators, echoing into the passageway.

The Manticore shrieked loudly and spun around almost instantaneously, and bolted away from the prisoners.

"Shit!" Marquez exclaimed. The prisoners began sprinting desperately after the creature, following its booming footsteps. "You don't need to run away, we're not here to hurt you!"

"It's not working Joey, fuck this!" Waters yelled before he knocked Miller and Marquez out of the way. He brought his rifle up to fire by nesting it firmly between his shoulder and his collar bone. Before Marquez could stop him, he opened fire. He let out fifteen shots towards the creature's hind legs. It let out a cry of agony, turned around, and began charging the prisoners. Feig pulled the pin out of a flashbang grenade and threw it towards the creature. Its cries were reduced to a high-pitched ringing, and the hallway was completely enveloped in a blinding blue light.

"Don't shoot! Shit, don't shoot!" Marquez yelled in vain, as Miller, Waters, and Feig all began firing at the

Manticore. It resumed its charge, seemingly unfazed by the rounds fired at it. Its feet shook the ground with every step, and its open mouth came at them once more. Waters dropped his pistol and readied a shotgun. He fired off two shells in succession.

"That's it, we're pulling the fuck out of here!" Marquez hollered.

"Ignore that order! Take the Manticore down! Now!" Schuck screamed uncharacteristically over the communicator.

"Fuck him, let's go! Back to the elevator, now!" Marquez insisted.

"Do not disengage! You almost have it!"

The Manticore swiped at the prisoners, its enormous paw took down a wall along with it. Marquez and Miller were knocked to the ground and covered in rubble. Waters and Feig quickly rushed over to pull them up. All they could see were its eyes glowing a few yards away from them. The Manticore let out a loud, hellish cry before it turned around and ran away from them again.

"Now's our chance! Back to the elevator!" Marquez yelled.

"DO NOT FOLLOW THAT ORD-" Wilkins tried to interject.

"Fuck you! We're getting out of here!" Miller cut him off.

The prisoners ran hurriedly towards the intersection where the elevator waited for them. Marquez quickly opened the elevator doors and corralled the other three prisoners in. He hurriedly followed them in and hit the switch to advance toward the surface.

The elevator hummed and jostled as they moved upwards towards the light of day. They weren't expecting what awaited them at the top. The doors opened and twelve soldiers awaited them with their rifles aimed directly at them. The prisoners put their hands up and dropped their weapons instinctually.

"Listen, I can expla-" Marquez began to utter as a group of soldiers walked towards him and beat him with the butts of their weapons.

"What the fuck do you think you're doing?!" Waters exclaimed. He was quickly restrained and beaten savagely by more of the soldiers. Miller and Feig got on their knees.

"Let them go man! There's no need to do this!" Miller pleaded, but it only brought their attention to him. The soldiers eventually dragged Feig over to the others and proceeded to ruthlessly beat all four of them. Marquez dipped in and out of consciousness. In those brief moments of clarity, all he could remember was the boot of one of the soldiers coming down onto his face. He wasn't sure how much time had gone by, but he couldn't see the position of the sun, as his blood was covering the visor of his helmet. He could feel himself being dragged through the leaves and grass. The pain in his face was so immense he wanted to scream, but his mouth was so swollen he could barely move it. He decided he didn't care to be conscious anymore and allowed himself to pass out for good.

***

Time blurred and dragged, and eventually, Marquez awoke in a familiar setting. He was straddled by fluorescent lights, and a busy medical team rushing around him. He caught a glimpse of the other prisoners in surgical beds across the room. He couldn't move his arms or head, as he was strapped into the surgical chair.

"Let me out of here," Marquez uttered through his battered, swollen face.

"Nurse, sedation please! Forty milligrams of propofol on a drip, please!" the doctor shouted. An anxious nurse hurried over and hooked up a bag to Marquez's surgical chair. He swiftly coasted back into unconsciousness.

Hours later, Marquez awoke, feeling hungover with an immeasurably painful throb in his face and head.

"Welcome back, mister Marquez," Schuck said with forced politeness.

"Schuck, I-" Marquez tried to reply.

"Don't waste your energy, and most importantly don't waste my time. Doctor, are the others awake yet?"

"Prisoners two and four are awake, three is still out." the doctor said nervously.

"Wake up mister Waters, would you? I need to debrief them."

"Sir, they should really still be resting. The soldiers beat them pretty badly."

"Am I correct in assuming that I'm hearing someone refuse my orders? Are we not surrounded by examples of what happens when people refuse my orders?"

"Sorry, sir, I'll wake up mister Waters at once, sir."

"Thank you."

The doctor rushed over to Waters' surgical bed and administered a stimulant to counteract the sedative effects of the propofol. Waters let out a panicked cry of pain as the stimulant not only woke him up but his nerve endings as well.

"Give him a mild pain reliever, but keep him coherent, would you doctor?"

"Y-yes sir," the doctor administered a mild painkiller to Waters.

"Do the rest as well, please. Leave mister Marquez to me though, understood?"

"Sir," the doctor said nervously.

Schuck drew the plastic curtain around Marquez's bed to a complete close, blocking any vision or audio between him and the other prisoners.

"Listen to me, mister Marquez. That little stunt that you pulled would have gotten anyone else killed on the spot. What my men did to you was mere child's play compared to what will happen if you disobey my direct orders again. Are we clear?" Schuck said in an angry whisper.

Marquez was in excruciating pain and his head fell limp. Schuck grabbed him firmly by his swollen, bloody, and bruised cheeks. Marquez let out a scream in agony. "Are we clear, mister Marquez?"

"Cl-clear... Chuck."

"Good. Let this be a lesson to you. You're lucky that you and your newfound friends are even alive, let alone still taking part in this mission," Schuck gazed directly into his eyes and a small, devilish grin broke out on Schuck's face. He drew the curtain open again and addressed the prisoners as a group. "Gentlemen, what you did was a clear and direct violation of your agreement in being here. Any further insubordination will not be tolerated."

"Ha! Agreement, he says. You hear that Feig? We have an agreement! Where's my copy of the contract, there, Chuck?" Waters quipped with a pained laugh.

"Yes, agreement. You were to be sentenced to death, but we gave you an out. You agreed to come here and help us contain the Manticore, and if you renege on that, we'll simply carry out your initial sentence," Schuck spoke with assertive self-importance.

"Chuck, the judge didn't really make it clear that we could have just chosen death. If I remember correctly, he said 'you've been chosen to take part in an alternative sentence', which means we didn't really agree to shit. You can dance around it all you want, but none of us are here by choice. We're just trying to survive."

"If you keep these antics up, you *won't* survive your next encounter with the Manticore."

"I never said we were trying to survive against the Manticore. We're trying to survive our time with you, pal," Waters began to laugh, but the pain in his ribs became unbearable, which brought him into a sharp coughing fit.

Schuck scoffed, "Think what you will, mister Waters, I'm not entertaining your philosophical propaganda any longer. Onto the business at hand. First, you disobeyed direct orders, and unless you want another trip to this room, that *won't* happen again. Secondly, our combat analytics are suggesting that the creature has adapted to the initial formula used in the batch of ammunition you've been using. Our research and development team has a new formula that will be more potent than the last, and you will be using it for your next sortie. If you balk at the creature the next time you engage, well... I'm sure you already know how that will go. Are we clear, gentlemen?"

Miller, Feig, and Waters nodded at him weakly.

"Mister Marquez?"

"I already told you earlier, Chuck. We're clear."

"Very well. You'll spend the next few days here recovering from the tussle you got in with squad eight. Once you've all recovered, we'll begin discussing your next deployment," Schuck quickly took off for the door, and turned around briefly to shoot a glance at Marquez, who immediately became uneasy.

The prisoners waited a few minutes to make sure Schuck was gone before attempting to speak again.

"D-do you think he's onto us?" Feig said nervously.

"There's nothing to be onto, I just didn't want to commit to an engagement that was bound to be a loss. You almost died once already, no use testing our luck again," Marquez said, widening his eyes to the best of his ability to signal to Feig. He didn't want to speak about their knowledge of the girl out in the open.

"Shit, I think we would have been better off fighting the fuckin' Manticore. Those pussies beat the shit out of us after we surrendered. Then again, they really do like to make examples out of dissenters," Waters groaned.

"Precisely. Which is why it's even more shocking we were even brought to this island. They should have just killed us..." Feig said defeated and with a pained grunt.

"No one's dying. Fuck, man... Waters already lost everything. We almost lost Feig. Miller's the closest thing to family I've got. We have to make it out of here. We'll just do what they say... contain the Manticore for them and get out of here," Marquez didn't believe his own words.

The other prisoners were silent for a few moments.

"Joey, you know they're not going to let us out of here alive. You're a good kid, and so is Miller, even if he's a pain in the ass sometimes," Waters said somberly. "It's nice to know that not every asshole in this country is apathetic, or even worse a fuckin' willing participant in the whole god damned circus."

"You're not too bad yourself. I mean, I got my ass kicked for trying to save you, so the least you could have done is say 'thanks'. But I'll take it," Marquez said with an aggrieved snigger. "Between being sent here in chains and the beating, I think I'm starting to see where you guys are coming from. Not that *I'd* want to be labeled a fringe lunatic, but I see why you're so pissed off."

"It's a hard pill to swallow, man, believe me. I struggled for a while... I had to challenge everything I was told to believe. I mean, we're born into it, so it's hard to imagine anything else, you know?" Waters' tone grew serious.

"Democracy is a nice notion. I used to think that I had a voice, and that the powers that be gave a damn... but, well... you see where we are now and how we got here," Feig fought to get the words out. "Most people just live in ignorance. Many of them do so willingly..."

"The whole damn thing is a joke. Fuckin' feds took over the hospitals, and not a single one of them has equipment like the one we're in right now. Goes to show where their fuckin' priorities are," Waters said angrily. "I knew we were fucked the day they announced they were taking over the media. It wasn't long after that they started assigning people jobs. Bit by bit they took over the whole fuckin' show, and for what?"

"The greater good," Feig said dryly and rolled his eyes weakly.

"What the fuck does that even mean?! What's good for me isn't necessarily good for Marquez, and what's good for him isn't necessarily good for Miller! The whole concept makes no fuckin' sense," Waters' rage allowed him to yell through the pain.

"Yet we're the weird ones," Feig again said dryly.

"You think if we took a vote, they'd let us leave?" Waters laughed.

"Easy, fellas, or you'll pop a stitch," Miller groaned.

"Joey, where'd you fuckin' find this guy?" Waters asked jokingly.

"I never told you about how I met Miller?" Marquez responded incredulously. "My parents brought me here from Costa Rica after the Partido Vanguardia Popular took over when I was a baby, and my family started to struggle. My parents owned a fruit market, but the PVP took over distribution of food. Everyone was told they had a 'guaranteed job.' My parents worked their asses off for that business just to be told they were going to back to what they did before," Marquez paused, as the swelling in his face made it difficult to speak. "They were already planning on moving to the United States, but they weren't planning on it being so soon. Luckily, they knew a guy with a boat, he did local shipments, fishing trips, stuff like that. My parents, me, and another family packed onto the boat and made our way towards Florida. We landed near Tallahassee because Tampa and Miami were popular for illegals at the time, and lots of immigrants were being caught and deported there. We stayed with a Cuban family for a few weeks while my dad was looking for work. They said that one of the neighbors tipped off the immigration agents, but they don't really know for sure. We had to run, so the Cuban family had to kick us out before they went to jail. Long story short, my parents did what they could to make some money and eventually made their way up to New Jersey. They didn't like to talk about that time, and I don't remember much of it. Every time I asked them, they'd deflect or just say that they're glad they got me here. I was 6 or 7 years old by the time we finally settled."

"Jesus Christ, I can only imagine what they went through," Waters said.

"They went through hell, but they wanted a better life. I miss them, but I'm glad they're not around to see how the country ended up. Just like back home."

"Shit, I didn't know they passed, I'm sorry."

"It's alright, it was long before any of this. My dad had a bad heart and they caught it too late. My mom missed him so much, she was never quite the same after he died. I think she wanted to die, too, you know? She passed a year later. Natural causes."

"I miss em' too, Joey. They were like my second family," Miller said with a hurt, saddened look.

"Shit, I'm rambling, guys. Sorry, yeah, so when we first got here, we didn't know anyone and my parents didn't speak English very well, but they found work and we got a little apartment. First thing they did was get me into school. My English was better than theirs because I grew up here, but that didn't stop people from picking on me. I was the new kid *and* I was the foreigner. Miller was bigger than most of the other kids and was the first one to even talk to me. He had my back when the other kids would call me names or if they tried to beat me up. We got our asses kicked a few times, but we kicked asses back in return. People eventually stopped fucking with us, and we've kind of been family ever since."

"Well look, if by some miracle we do make it out of here, let me buy everyone a fuckin' drink. If it pleases the crown, of course." Waters said as he once again laughed in pain.

The prisoners took turns telling jokes and sharing stories with one another. As the night went on, they eventually fell asleep, one by one. Waters was last, and he couldn't help but reflect on his own life after hearing about the troubles the rest of the group went through. He wept quietly to himself as he thought about his wife and children. He vividly remembered his wife fading away, and how his children cried as they were carried off in a police vehicle. Eventually, however, he began to smile. He put away the dark memories and thought about the great ones he had of them. Despite the situation he found himself in, he knew he had some good people to talk to. With dried tears on his bruised and bloodied face, he drifted into sleep.

***

"If the natural tendencies of mankind are so bad that it is not safe to permit people to be free, how is it that the tendencies of these organizers are always good? Do not the legislators and their appointed agents also belong to the human race? Or do they believe that they themselves are made of a finer clay than the rest of mankind?"
— Frédéric Bastiat

Chapter 7 - The Evil That Men Do

After a few days of recovery, Marquez could see and speak without being in pain. His face had mostly healed with only a few scabs and bruises remaining. The prisoners sat at their table, eating their breakfast as if it were any other day.

"When do you think they're going to make us go back down there?" Miller said.

"Don't know, but now that we're out of those fucking hospital beds, I guess it could be any day now," Waters replied.

"As much as I'd like to leave this place as soon as humanly possible... I hope they give us a bit more time off. The sharp pain is mostly gone, but my entire upper body is one giant, dull ache," Marquez chimed in.

"I feel that, Joey. Damn, do I feel that," Waters said, shaking his head.

Brief static popped over the intercom, "Mister Marquez and mister Feig, report to strategic operations immediately after your meal," Schuck's voice had its signature professional sound but with the subtle anger that Marquez recognized from their encounter in the medical bay.

"What the fuck? Why just you two?" Waters said throwing his hands up in the air and gesturing towards Marquez and Feig.

"I don't know, but it can't be good. Shit!" Marquez slammed his fork down. "Let's just go, Feig. I'm not too hungry anymore, and I'd rather just see what the prick wants now than stew about it."

Feig nodded, gently placed his fork down and began to walk towards the door, with Marquez joining him.

The walk along the catwalks was as tense as it had ever been. *He's onto us... he's gotta be*, Marquez thought. *Either that, or...*

"Do you think he's onto us?" Feig said, interrupting Marquez's thought.

"I don't know, honestly. Why else would he single us out, though?"

"I don't have a very good feeling... Then again, something felt wrong from the moment we stepped onto the island."

"Maybe we'll finally get a straight answer this time, but I'm not holding my breath. We're almost there. If he asks us about... if he asks us anything, we don't know, alright?"

Feig nodded.

As they approached the strategic operations office, the door hissed open and Schuck walked out, extending his right hand toward the open doorway, inviting them in.

"Have a seat, gentlemen," Schuck said as he walked over to what looked like a small footlocker opposite the table. They heard a small hiss and clanking but couldn't see what Schuck was doing. He turned around and revealed two small tumblers with cold whiskey stones and a clear, brown liquid filled half way to the top. Schuck placed the glasses in front of Marquez and Feig and made a small gesture towards them, encouraging them to drink.

"It's a little early, Schuck. I appreciate it, but I think I'm okay for now," Marquez said as politely as possible. While Marquez spoke, Schuck fixed himself a glass and sat down opposite them.

"Suit yourself, but it's not poisoned or laced. If you're concerned about our treatment of mister Feig, it was completely voluntary, and I would never resort to such tasteless tactics. Besides, that's not what you're here for," Schuck replied, gently sipping his drink periodically.

"What exactly are we here for? Sir?" Feig said.

"You're here because of the girl," Schuck's voice was slightly muffled, as his glass was raised to his lips. He then chewed on some of the small bits of ice from the final sip. Marquez and Feig didn't flinch.

"What girl? The one in the medical bay? I didn't know you guys had human resources here, it's just lonely, Schuck, I didn't really mean anything by it! Plus you had me all doped up on painkillers!" Marquez joked.

"Mister Marquez, you can cut the act. Before you say anything, mister Feig, I'm well aware that you know too. I actually wanted to apologize to you both. Please, drink. It's impolite to let a man drink alone." Feig looked to Marquez with a puzzled look in his eyes and Marquez returned the favor. They reluctantly raised their glasses and chased the taste of cafeteria food down with the whiskey, which, much to Marquez's chagrin, was delicious. "So, gentlemen, first things first. I'd like to formally apologize for the mistreatment you received at the end of your last mission. After analyzing the data, we found that your chance for success in that particular encounter was somewhere around thirteen percent. Pulling your team out was the right call. Admittedly, I was angry, and I should have never let them hurt you the way they did."

"Right, they should have only hurt us a little, not a lot, right?" Marquez said sarcastically.

Ignoring Marquez's response, Schuck continued, "Secondly, I'm sorry that we didn't tell you the whole story from the beginning, but we were afraid that it would have affected your judgment on missions if you knew that the Manticore was indeed human in origin."

"Doesn't affect me as much as being forced into this mission and then lied to," Marquez responded with scorn.

"Mister Marquez, I understand your frustration, but try to see it from our perspective. If we told you that up front would you have been willing to fire upon it when you first encountered it?"

"Her."

"Excuse me?"

"Fire on her when we first encountered her. And you're right, I wouldn't have, because why the fuck would I want to shoot a scared, naked, young girl?"

"I'm getting to that. I wasn't lying to you when I said that it was a Chinese bio weapon developed during the war, we-"

"She."

"Mister Marquez, we can sit here and argue semantics until the apocalypse, but please, may I continue?"

Marquez scoffed and rolled his eyes.

"As I was saying, we captured it... her, during a mission in the Russian theater. We were able to follow a trail of files to the original source of the experiment, but by the time our forces arrived, they had purged their data and flooded the laboratory that they developed her in. As such, the secrets of her abilities were lost, but we still had her. If we can analyze her DNA and cell structure to find what changed, we could potentially find a way to reverse the effects on her and find a way to grant these abilities to our own soldiers without any adverse effects."

"Oh, fuck off! You're telling me that you want to help her, but in the same breath saying that you want to use her as a fucking guinea pig so you can make super soldiers?!" Marquez yelled. Feig looked noticeably uncomfortable.

"It's a matter of national defense! The war may be over, but the world is still reeling from its effects. Extremist groups have appeared in South Korea, Hong Kong, and even a cell in Turkmenistan. Local warlords that are using their compromised economies and weakened governmental presence from the Chinese invasion to stir up dissent! If we don't put a stop to it now-"

"So, you want to step in and save the day with monstrous super soldiers so you can control them like you did with South America and Canada? Jesus Christ, you're trying to run the whole fucking world, aren't you?!" Marquez yelled, standing up from his seat.

"These people have no direction, and no purpose! If we don't do something about it, no one else will, and they would be injured, or worse, killed! It's for the greater well-being of mankind!" Schuck stood from his seat to look into Marquez's eyes as he delivered his response.

"So, you don't want them to be killed by extremists but it's okay to be killed by you?! Do you even listen to yourself?!"

"I see the bigger picture, mister Marquez, and I'm a realist. The masses could never be left to their own devices! If we don't-"

"If you don't what?! 'Liberate' them and then rule them with an army of monsters?"

"Listen to me, if you want to help that girl, then SIT! You can question our strategic choices after the fact, but if you really want to help this girl, then listen to me!" Schuck grabbed everyone's glasses and prepared another drink. He put down their tumblers with a loud thud, causing the whiskey to rock back and forth, liquid tension barely keeping it in the glass. "I understand that you find yourselves in an... odd situation here, but please, help us help you. We want to help the girl as much as you do, but we also want to make sure that she didn't suffer through whatever trials the Chinese government subjected her to were in vain."

Marquez sat with his arms crossed, staring down at nothing, breathing heavily with rage.

"You're really going to help her? You're not trying to kill her?"

"Mister Marquez, she may be the single most important person in the world right now. To kill her would be a tragedy. She deserves to go back to a normal life, and we can help give her that while simultaneously gaining priceless insight into human physiology. If we were trying to kill her, we wouldn't have engineered the ammunition how we have. We have a new version of it for you to use on your next deployment. It won't kill her. It will simply slow down her regeneration enough to contain her safely."

Feig looked at Marquez, who was still trembling with rage.

Marquez's thoughts raced, and his rage grew until he finally accepted Schuck's proposition.

"FUCK! Fine! Fine, but I'm telling you right now, that if we're at risk down there again, and I make the call to pull us out, you better have your guys kill us, because I swear to fucking God that if we're greeted by another welcoming committee, we won't be throwing our weapons down. Do you understand me?"

"Loud and clear, mister Marquez. You all will be deploying tomorrow morning, so get your team together, and prepare yourselves however you need to. Again, I'm sorry for how we had to handle things."

Marquez didn't respond, stood up quickly, and proceeded directly for the door. Feig followed immediately after.

***

Marquez was walking so fast it bordered on a jog. Feig scrambled to catch up. "Hey! Joey, wait a second!" Feig said, catching his breath, "Listen... I think Schuck is bullshitting us. Everything in there... it was an act."

"Feig, I'm inclined not to trust the guy either, but maybe if we play along this time, we can actually help her."

"I'm telling you, he doesn't want to help her, and he's not going to. I... I can't-" Feig was getting angry at himself for tripping over his words, "I guess you could call it a gut feeling, but I'm just- I'm asking you to trust me."

Marquez pushed the heels of his hands into his eyes in exasperation, slid them down over his face and let out a large sigh. "Fine, but we have to get back and tell the guys. Everyone's got to be on the same page if we're going to figure out a way to get her out."

The walk back was completely silent. Marquez racked his brain, envisioning countless possible scenarios and outcomes for their next plunge into the sub level. Feig began to feel increasingly unwell, as a fire began to burn in his chest.

Has to be some sort of tissue damage from when I was attacked, Feig thought, *the treatment was good, but a wound that severe was bound to have some lasting effects. I can't let it get in the way of getting out of here... I can't let them down.*

When they arrived back at the cafeteria minutes later, Marquez stormed in, going directly to Waters.

"Let me get a smoke." he said, as he held back his rage and anxiety.

"You alright, man?" Waters said with visible concern on his face as he frantically pulled the pack of cigarettes from his chest pocket.

"Not really. We've got some shit to go over."

Waters pulled the lighter out, and tapped the package with two swift smacks, raising a group of cigarettes out. He took one and placed it in Marquez's extended hand and took another and placed it between his own lips. "Let's take a walk, then. Feig! Miller! Smoke?" he shouted, as Feig had meandered over to Miller, who was seated on a bench over by the doorway that led to the bunks and was struggling in removing the pivot pin from his rifle for a teardown and cleaning.

"Huh? Yeah, gimme a sec, I'm just trying to get this piece of shit apart. There's grime all over this fucking thing," Miller hollered back.

Marquez's head jerked towards them, but before he could angrily bark at him, Waters yelled back, "Come on Miller, you can ruin that rifle any other time you want, let's go burn one. Feig, you too."

Marquez knew that his anger shouldn't have been directed at Miller or anyone in the room for that matter. Despite being almost blinded with rage, he appreciated that Waters was able to recognize the mistake he was about to make and gave him a thankful nod. Marquez and Waters began walking

162

quickly towards the door and lit their cigarettes before getting outside. Miller jogged over to catch up, while Feig followed behind at a far slower pace. Feig rubbed his chest with his right hand. As they got outside, they saw Marquez and Waters leaning up against the wall. Marquez took a long drag and exhaled through his nose forcefully.

"So, what's going on?" Waters asked gently.

"Schuck knows about the girl."

"Jesus Christ. So you guys really weren't seeing shit. What, did he catch a glimpse of her from our combat footage?"

"No, that motherfucker has known from the *beginning*! He didn't tell us because he was afraid we wouldn't be willing to shoot at her if we knew it was person."

"Wait, wait, so what the fuck does that mean?" Miller said as the cigarette flapped in his mouth, which threw ash in his face.

"It means that the Chinese government didn't take a fucking panda and turn it into a monster, they took a *girl* and turned her into a fucking *weapon*."

Miller placed his left hand on his forehead and ran his fingers through his hair with wide eyes as he took in the gravity of the situation. "Which means they want us to do their fuckin' dirty work and put her down?"

"That's the thing, Schuck said they don't want to kill her, they just want to get her contained so they can figure out what they did to her, keep the research, and *cure* the girl."

"Don't tell me you bought that bullshit!" Waters yelled confoundedly.

"Feig doesn't believe him either, but think about it, the ammo they gave us wasn't meant to kill her. The one thing he did say from the very beginning is that they're trying to *subdue* her, not *kill* her!"

"You're fucking kidding yourself! You think they're not going to kill her off once she's no longer useful?"

"What other choice do we have?! We can either take his word for it and hope that it's our one chance to get her, and *us*, mind you, out of here alive, or we can just roll over and take the execution! If we complete our mission, they get what they want, and if we're extremely fucking lucky, we get to go home, and so does she."

"Ruby Ridge? Waco siege? Any of those ring a bell?!"

Marquez averted his eyes.

"Didn't think so, they don't teach you that shit in school. A hundred and fifty years ago, the same kind of people like Schuck didn't think twice about murdering their own people over nothing. You think a girl, who's imprisoned on an island that the entire populace of the country doesn't know is a fucking *research installation*, is going to be set free and handed a new start just because some soft-hand prick in a dress uniform sold you a promise of good will? Christ, Joey, you're smarter than that!"

"So what do we do, Phil? How the fuck are we supposed to get her out of there if they're just going to execute us all regardless?" Marquez snapped, yelling over Waters.

Waters grunted and bashed his hands against the wall in anger. The group fell silent for a few moments.

"We have to talk to her, like Joey tried to before," Miller said with confidence.

"Yeah? And what exactly do we say, huh? 'Sorry you got used by the Chinese government, but we're here to set you free?' What fuckin' planet are you on?" Waters said angrily.

"We have to talk to her because she's the only way that *any* of us are getting out of here," Miller responded firmly.

"So what, we're supposed to use her just like they are? As a fucking weapon?" Waters seethed.

"Look, I know it's fucked up, but... yeah, basically. I don't *want* to use her, but if she's enough of a threat to keep Schuck and his pals scared, then we don't have any other choice. If we tried to do anything ourselves, sure, we *might* be able to put up a good fight, but they'd overwhelm us with numbers and firepower. She knows the sub level, and she can turn into... Look, I don't like it either, Christ only knows what she's been through already, but it might be our only chance. Either we try to work with her and have a chance of getting the fuck off of this island, or we play along with Schuck and get all of us - her included - killed one way or another."

Marquez was visibly distressed. He knew that Miller was right, and what was worse was that they had to convince the girl to behave like the weapon she was intended to be. He felt physically uncomfortable at the thought of it, but he knew it was their only option, and hers.

"Fuck. Miller's right. They're not letting us leave alive unless we fight our way out."

Waters walked over to Miller and stared him directly in the eyes. He let out a heavy sigh. "I don't know about you guys, but I need another cigarette," Waters pulled the pack out and distributed one to each of the prisoners. They smoked in silence, knowing exactly what it was that they had to do, and that after this, there was no going back. No more daytime conversations on magnetically masked communicators. No more cardboard and cat shit meals. No more smoke breaks. They knew that the very next day would change everything, for better or for worse.

***

No one slept particularly well that night. Each of their minds raced, they thought deeply about the consequences of their next deployment to the sub level. They all tossed and turned through the night. Feig had an especially hard time, as the burning in his chest seemed to grow worse as the night went on and his anxiety became more apparent. When the sun rose and the klaxon resounded to call them to action, they were all already awake, having not uttered a word to one another.

They marched reservedly to strategic operations to check in with Schuck, without so much as a peep or a sigh. Their own quietness matched that of the island itself. Their walking was even so that it barely disturbed the catwalk, their steps reduced to small thuds on the swaying metal. As always, Schuck awaited them with an open door and an extended arm.

"Please, have a seat, gentlemen," Schuck said gravely.

The prisoners piled in, sat in their respective chairs, and remained motionless as Schuck began to give his brief.

"I'm sure you all didn't sleep very well. To be frank, I didn't get much sleep myself. I understand that this mission is getting to you, and now that the circumstances have changed, it hasn't gotten any easier. Yes, it is indeed a girl down there. One we're very much interested in helping. We've prepared a new version of the ammunition you've used in your previous mission. It should be much more effective in subduing the Manticore without harming her. If you can subdue her today, you will be free tomorrow, I promise you that."

Not one of the prisoners flinched or mumbled.

"The new ammunition is in the armory. Gear up, and head to the main gate by zero nine hundred. With any luck, this will be your last venture into the sub level, and this will be that girl's last day trapped in there."

Marquez and the other prisoners stood up wordlessly and made their way to the armory. Everyone stocked up on magazines, shells, hand thrown explosives, and concussive devices. Occasionally, the prisoners' eyes would line up, with unspoken wishes of luck being sent and received by each party involved. *It feels like Knightsbridge all over again,* Marquez pondered, *but if I can't get the girl out, I guess I could always take myself out of the equation.*

The prisoners waited patiently outside of the main gate. The guard posted there was devoid of his usual devilish smirk. The tension seemed to be palpable not only for the prisoners but for the entire island. The eerie silence was punctuated by the quiet from the otherwise chatty assemblage of inmates. The guard kept checking the time indication at the top right of his heads-up display, and at zero nine hundred exactly, he threw the switch, causing the familiar hydraulic hiss of the gate, which opened the way to what could have been the prisoners' last time going through it.

They made their way to the squeaky hatch and without hesitation pried the handle and lifted it open. Marquez began his descent, swiftly followed by Miller, then Waters, and lastly Feig.

The musty, dirt smell permeated their nostrils, but this time it smelled different. The ambient hum of the sub level was overtaken by the sound of Marquez pulling back the slide on his rifle, which he let slam back into position. The bolt carrier's metallic grind brought a round into the chamber. The other prisoners repeated this action, and they began their journey into the familiar but no less fearsome territory.

The ground beneath their boots squished and squelched from the excess water and overgrowth. Drips of water echoed in the distance, like leaky faucets in a concert hall. The silence highlighted the drops to the point of making them sound booming and loud. Marquez began to breathe heavily with apprehension and nerves. Waters' brow began to sweat as he watched the rear and listened intently for any signs of the girl. The dust particles glistened in the beams of light emanating from the flashlights attached to their rifles, dancing in the air as the prisoners moved around the tight corridor. As they approached the corner ahead of them, Marquez threw his hand up, which signaled everyone to stop. He peeked around the corner carefully, and quickly darted his head back to safety. He then peeked again, this time with his rifle to illuminate the hallway. Opened doors, battered office furniture, rubble, and debris peppered the hallway.

While Marquez was being extremely diligent in preparing for the group to move up, Waters and Feig heard a sound that chilled them to their bones. The low, otherworldly grumble of the Manticore reverberated off of the walls around them. Feig jumped and turned around, and his flashlight illuminated the large eyes which gazed back at him. She had been following them at a distance since they set foot in the sub level, walking on cat's paws so as not to make a sound.

Marquez jolted his body around as soon as he could, and began yelling with his hands - and weapon - up in the air.

"WAIT! Wait! Wait! We don't want to hurt you, please! Guys, put your fucking weapons down, now!" He hollered, which resonated through the halls. Waters raised his weapon, perhaps a bit too abruptly, and the Manticore reared up in preparation to defend.

"No! No, I'm not going to hurt you! I'm putting my weapon down, okay?" Waters said in a panic, as sweat dripped into his eyes. "I'm sorry. I'm putting the gun down, okay?"

Miller and Feig slowly raised their weapons up in a non-threatening way and gently placed them onto the soggy, mud covered floor.

"My name is Joseph Marquez, remember me? These guys here are Waters, Feig, and Miller. We want to get you out of here safely and alive, okay? We don't want to hurt you."

The Manticore chittered suspiciously, and produced a sequence of short, airy barks.

"We know that you're a girl, and we know that you don't want to be here. We're unarmed, and we don't want anyone else to get hurt. I don't even know if you can fucking understand English... Are you able to... fuck, how do I say this?" Marquez began gesturing with his hands, as he tried to create an animation that would convey to her that he wants her to change into her human form. "Can you do that? Can you become human again?"

The Manticore let out a shrill, piercing shriek for a brief moment, and then began to groan as if it was in pain. Before their very eyes, the monster in front of them began to pulsate and move in sharp, jittery motions. Quickly, the form began to take the shape of a girl.

The prisoners looked on in awe as the hulking beast of hardened flesh morphed into a young woman, curled up on the floor, naked. Her black hair rested gracefully over her shoulders, despite the dirt and grime from the unknown amount of time she had been down here. She slowly began to stand up, not even thinking of covering herself, as the tension of the situation superseded any instincts of courtesy.

The prisoners averted their eyes. She couldn't have been any older than twenty-three or twenty-four. Tears began to streak down her face. She was hunted down there for so long, and she finally felt she had the possibility of freedom.

"It's okay, it's okay," Marquez said, looking directly into her eyes. "We're not here to hurt you."

She began to weep uncontrollably, and collapsed back to the floor. Her knees landed in a puddle of dirty water, which splashed it up onto her thighs.

"Miller, see if you can find a blanket or something to cover her with. Check one of the offices. There has to be something."

Miller nodded, still in shock at what had just transpired before his very eyes and took off hastily towards the nearest office.

Waters and Feig stood in place, with their hands in the air, completely stunned. Marquez sat on the ground with one knee lifted up, upon which he rested his forearm. *What the fuck is the next step? We've got her here, as a human, but what now...* he wondered anxiously.

His thoughts were abruptly interrupted as multiple instances of subtle glows came tramping around the corner behind where the girl sat on the ground. Feig saw them first. He grabbed his rifle, and began opening fire.

Schuck had sent a separate team down without their knowledge.

As the first round left the chamber, Marquez leapt up into position and scrambled to shoulder his rifle.

"No!" he shouted, but it was deafened by the gunfire. The girl locked eyes with him, tears were still damp on her face, and she gave him a look of disenchantment. In what felt like a single heartbeat, the girl's body had crumpled, shifted, and rearranged. She had turned back into the Manticore as Schuck's men began to open fire on her. She felt as if she had been fooled. She felt it was all a ruse, and that they faked it all to get her to let her guard down, and in one instantaneous swipe of her claw, Feig's torso had been flayed open, once again, to ribbons. Waters rushed over to his bleeding friend. He ignored the gunfire, as Miller had made his way back and began

172

returning fire to Schuck's men. Feig's eyes were glassy, and blood babbled from his mouth. His armor was ripped and frayed, and his exposed flesh was leaking blood at a rate that no amount of surgery could fix.

This is it, Feig thought, *penance.* He looked at Waters, and while he was unable to speak, he contemplated powerfully one final thought, as if to hope that Waters would receive it through some sort of telepathy, *set her free.*

Waters' eyes welled up with fury and anguish. Marquez and Miller continued firing from behind them as Waters crawled over to his weapon. Amidst the din and carnage, a rapid beeping could be heard coming from Feig's direction.

Feig mustered up a smile as his eyes closed. A loud explosion came from his chest, which blanketed the corridor in flesh and viscera. Waters frantically wiped his visor in vain until ultimately, he took his helmet off. The gunfire had ceased, and the dust had begun to settle. A few scraps of Feig remained in the location he landed after getting mauled by the Manticore. Waters collapsed to his knees and stared at the smoldering rubble and gore that used to be his best friend. Feig's blood dripped from the ceiling. Waters retched violently. Miller gripped his weapon ferociously, though his magazine was empty. Marquez sprinted to make sure the girl was okay, and as he ran past Waters, his eyes widened when he saw the visceral smudge of what used to be Feig. The girl was back in her human form, covered in blood, but he couldn't tell now whether it was hers, Feig's, or the soldiers'. The bodies of Schuck's team littered the corner, which was covered in debris and blood from the explosion.

Marquez arrived at the girl, and took his helmet off. He discarded it to the side, and threw his weapon down shortly after. The helmet thudded on one of the soldier's corpses. He gently placed his hands on her cheeks and turned her face towards his. With a wounded moan, her eyes lazily began to open.

Chapter 8 - Killers

There was a brief moment of silence, as the ringing in their ears faded. Marquez held the girl's face in his hands, and her eyes widened. He brushed the dirt and debris from her cheeks with his thumb gently. Her eyes darted around the room, taking in the gore strewn about, most specifically, the dark red puddle of flesh and rock from the explosion that emanated from Feig's chest. She pulled herself away from Marquez, but was unable to stand, and she quickly collapsed to the ground and fought to keep her eyes open. As Marquez began to move towards her to make sure she didn't run, the silence was shattered by the familiar static of their communicators.

"Gentlemen..." Schuck's voice was trembling with a violent, monstrous rage, despite his best efforts to hide it, "Would you care to explain why you killed one of our best units on the island? You were sent down there for the SOLE purpose of retrieving the gi-" Schuck was cut off, as Commander Wilkins had muscled his way to the communicator.

"You sons of whores better make any last wishes you have, because you won't be leaving this fucking island alive, with or without the girl! Do you fucking hear me? For the first time in my career I actually questioned my superiors when they suggested we employ you fucking terrorists, you enemies of the country *I swore an oath to protect*! If I had my way, I'd come down there myself and flay you all alive and broadcast it to the god damned FNN to show those of your ilk what happens when you bite the hand that fucking feeds you!"

Wilkins' voice began to crack as he screamed at the prisoners, Marquez bided his time and interjected after Wilkins finished his rant.

"With all due respect, commander" Marquez said, drawling, "you sent a secondary fireteam down without so much as a heads up, and they opened fire on the girl that Schuck said he was trying to fucking protect! That's why Feig opened fire and we followed suit. You want to play the victim, go ahead, but we were told that we would be able to-"

Wilkins decided he had had enough, and in childish, angry retaliation, interjected. "I don't give a flying fuck what you were told! Your mission was to help us get the Manticore under control, and instead you slaughtered an entire team of good soldiers! And for that you won't get the courtesy of execution! Oh, no, you pissants, you'll get to see one of the other functions of Petty Island, and I'm going to see to it personally," Wilkins' tone grew more sinister as he spoke. His voice decrescendoed into a malevolent, gravelly groan, as if he were speaking through painfully gritted teeth.

"You know what? It's obvious that neither of you want to listen to reason. Fuck this. We're done," Marquez said, angrily ripping the communicator from the back of his helmet. He then walked over to where Waters threw his helmet and destroyed his communicator as well.

"Think about what you're doing, we can still-" Schuck's voice echoed from Miller's helmet, which Marquez promptly ripped off of him and destroyed the communicator as well.

In a blind panic, Miller swung his fist with all of his might and hit Marquez directly in the jaw. The pain spread through Marquez's face like a shockwave and knocked him to the ground. He landed in a puddle of blood, the origin of which was not discernable at this point.

"You just guaranteed our fucking death sentence, you asshole!" Miller yelled and flung a kick at the downed Marquez, which hit him in his chest plate while Marquez tried to rub his jaw to ease the thunderous pain throbbing in the left side of his face. "What the fuck are we supposed to do now, huh? They're going to throw everyone they've got at us and throw our bullet ridden corpses in the fucking Delaware!" Miller let out a loud grunt of anger and placed his hands akimbo on his head, pacing rapidly and breathing heavily.

"They..." Marquez struggled to get the words out, and the pain gave him the slur of a drunkard. "They were going to kill us anyway, Miller."

"No! We could have still worked SOMETHING out. We have the girl. That's all they want, and you fucking destroyed our only way of talking to them without getting a bullet between the eyes!"

Waters came from the darkness, like a shadow. His eyes glowed from the small bit of ambient light coming from the pile of dead soldiers, their head lamps aiming upwards.

"Marquez is right. We had a death sentence the second we set foot on this island... we tried to tell you... Feig and I..."

"Listen, Phil, I-" Marquez was still struggling to speak.

"Don't. I don't wanna even hear it. It's not your fault, so stuff your sorries up your ass, alright?" Waters quivered with a visible, violent rage. His body was like a volcano about to erupt, and the other two prisoners took notice, keeping their distance.

"Miller, you were the one who said we had to talk to her to get out of here! This whole thing was your fucking idea!" Marquez angrily reminded him.

"I know! I know... I just... I don't want to fucking die, man." Miller sounded fearful and overwhelmed.

The group fell silent for a while, and the drips of blood onto the wet, dank floor resonated in the tight halls of the sub level. Marquez heard a small whimper, followed by a stifled weeping.

"Why... why won't you just kill me?" the girl spoke as tears streamed down her face.

Marquez looked at Waters, and then quickly at Miller, stunned at what he just heard.

"You speak English?!" Marquez blurted out loudly.

The girl looked as astonished as Marquez at the notion that they were surprised she spoke English.

"Why won't you kill me?!" she screamed shrilly, the corridors amplified her shriek, paining the prisoners.

"We're not here to kill you... we want to get you out of here. Safely. We want to get out of here too..." Marquez replied gently, with his hands raised so as to show he wasn't a threat, knowing very well she could transform and kill them all in mere moments if she so chose.

"Why did you kill the others? You're dressed like they are..." She whimpered, and quickly covered her bare skin with nearby scraps of armor.

"We're not soldiers. We're prisoners..."

The girl stared back at him with a confused look on her face.

"We were all supposed to be executed, but they sent us here to retrieve a monster they called the Manticore... to retrieve *you*..."

"Then... who were the others?" she said with anger in her voice.

"Those were soldiers, we didn't know they were coming down here with us. We were told we could get you out alive and safe. As for any others that came before us... I, uh... I don't know how long they've been using federal prisoners to try to kill you, but we definitely aren't the first..." Marquez said somberly.

The girl's confusion turned into horror as she placed her hands over her trembling lips. Her voice was muffled when she spoke, "The other one... he was another prisoner?"

"Yes," Marquez said.

Waters immediately spoke over him, "And a friend." His fist clenched as he uttered the words.

The girl began to cry uncontrollably as she realized that many of the people she had killed were most likely here against their will, and given no context to the creature they were to kill. She leaned forward, dropped the armor covering her to the ground, and her back arched as she retched violently onto the moldy floor of the sub level.

"They planted a fuckin' bomb in his chest," Waters said dryly.

The other prisoners said nothing.

"It was an insurance policy. One they decided to cash in on. I fuckin' warned you about playing along with these assholes! FUCK!" Waters stormed off into the darkness again to soothe his rage.

"The surgery, after he got clawed up the first time... Jesus Christ, Joey they turned him into a fucking weapon too!" Miller stated in disbelief.

"I know..."

"None of this would have happened if it wasn't for me... you should have just killed me." The girl said, her face still dripped with vomit.

"No. They're the reason you're here, and they're the ones that brought us here. How could you have known? You were acting out of self-defense. We were too, but we didn't want to kill you. Do you remember the first time we saw you? When you attacked Feig?"

The girl was silent.

"I saw you... I saw you as you really are, and I followed you into that room. Once I knew that you were a person and not just some Chinese bio-weapon, I just... I couldn't. I couldn't just kill you, even if it meant they'd let us go, which it's clear now they're not going to."

"If I..." the girl sniffled, "If I didn't hurt your friend, they wouldn't have put a bomb inside him..."

"You can't think like that. You didn't know... and neither did we."

The girl began to cry harder than before. She felt violated, lied to, and worse, she felt like a monster. Not just the one she was capable of turning into, but a killer. A murderer. Marquez looked around the corridor and found a large piece of torn clothing among the debris. He wasn't sure of where it came from, but he assumed it was once hers and had gotten torn to shreds during a defensive transformation. He brought it to her and gave it to her to cover herself. She wept into the soiled, tattered cloth, and Marquez sat down next to her and placed a hand on her shoulder. He gently pulled her head onto him. She sobbed quietly. Miller sat on the floor on the other side of the intersection, leaned up against a wall. He stared blankly into the dark hallway and kept his rifle close by. He was terribly afraid that Schuck's men would be coming any minute now.

***

As the hours passed by, the girl eventually fell asleep from exhaustion. Shortly after, Marquez followed suit. Miller, gripped by anxiety, fought it as best he could, but soon succumbed to the call of sleep after Marquez. It wasn't a good sleep. It was a shallow, fearful sleep. Miller barely awoke to hear the sound of rocks thudding against each other and the gentle scratches of footsteps on the floor. In a panic, he roused himself and grabbed the rifle next to him. He pulled the charging handle and ejected the round he had left in the chamber. It was a bad habit that Marquez had once scolded him for during the war.

"Relax, Miller. It's me." Miller recognized the voice. Waters sounded calmer than he ever had been since they met.

"What are you doing?" Miller asked, dazed from being half awake, and from an anxious sleep.

Waters didn't respond. He continued stacking rocks in a large pile, close to a foot and a half high, which formed a small ziggurat shape. Miller decided not to press the issue but didn't have the energy yet to stand up, and so he watched. Waters stacked the stones carefully with distinct calculation. He'd curse under his breath when they fell down or fell and took other rocks with them. After a few minutes, the construction was complete, and Waters once again set off into the darkness. He returned a few seconds later with Feig's helmet and scraps of his armor, covered in dust, dirt, and viscera. Waters sat and patiently, methodically cleaned the dirt from the helmet. Then he moved onto what was left of the armor. Once everything was cleaned to his liking, he placed the armor leaned up against the front of the small stone ziggurat, and finally, he gently placed the helmet atop its peak, making sure not to knock over the construction.

"He deserved better than this, but I guess it's better than nothin'," Waters said without being asked. "It's a grave. Couldn't very well bury a puddle, and I doubt they'd give us the time and opportunity to dig a hole. Plus, we'd just end up back in this fuckin' place."

Miller was surprised that Waters was able to retain his sense of humor given the situation, but deep down, he knew that it was a defense mechanism. Defense from the agonizing grief that was burning inside him. Miller knew better than to reply, choosing instead to nod.

"How are they? Marquez and the girl?" Waters asked. The concern in his voice was overwhelmingly genuine, almost saccharine.

"Still sleeping. Christ knows how, but still sleeping."

"I haven't slept a wink. I couldn't. Had to make sure Feig was taken care of first. I'm sure you're wondering, but no, I didn't run into any of Schuck's men, and I haven't heard a God damned thing so far. I think they're waiting. What for, I don't fuckin' know, but they're waiting."

"Good news, in a way, I guess."

"Yeah. Yeah..." Waters trailed off.

Miller wanted to keep Waters' mind occupied, to keep him from thinking about Feig. He knew it would most likely be in vain, but he wanted to try.

"So, what do you think she's dreaming about? Does she even still dream? Christ knows what kind of effect it has on her... all that genetic shit..."

"I don't know, but I'm curious too. Does she even remember who she is?"

"She speaks English. I don't know if you heard her, but she speaks English."

"Yeah, I heard. Wasn't too surprised, though. Ever since the war, most of the Chinese spoke English, at least enough to curse us out. A good bit of them spoke it well. It was the language of business, after all. That of course was before the mass embargoes. Shit," Waters spat.

"That's true, but still... I wonder if she dreams of her home?"

"Provided she still has one."

"Yeah... I almost wish I could, like, see her dreams, you know?"

"I thought the same thing, years ago. I told you about my wife. She got sick. There was a long period of time where she wasn't talking anymore. She wasn't awake anymore. I wished I could step into her dreams so I could see. I wanted to make sure she was dreaming of good things. I didn't even care at that point whether or not I could talk to her. I just wanted to make sure she wasn't suffering in her sleep too."

"Phil, for what it's worth-"

"It's not worth shit, Miller. I already told Marquez, and I'll tell you, I don't want to hear a fucking apology, do you understand?"

Waters pulled out an absolutely dilapidated pack of cigarettes and handed one to Miller who grabbed it without a second thought. Waters took his own and they took turns lighting them, making sure to be as quiet as possible.

Miller nodded, and looked over at the still sleeping Marquez, and the girl covered with the soiled, tattered cloth.

Chapter 9 - Innocent Exile

"Hey, Denise!" a voice called out to her from the other side of the Friendship Arch on 10th street. She was in Chinatown, in Center City, Philadelphia. Her home.

"Peter! I'm on my way to work. Did you still want to meet up later? There was a show at the Troc tonight, remember?"

"Oh, I didn't forget. I picked up the tickets for us already, so we won't have to worry about waiting in line."

"That's perfect! Thank you! And come see me on my lunch break! Are you starting late today?"

"Yeah, I don't start until three, so I'll come by around noon. We'll go to that Indian spot around the corner you've been wanting to go to."

"Awesome, I'll see you then!"

Denise was excited for the concert, and was dreading having to go to work. She tried to take off, but two of the other staff members had called out sick. It was the middle of January, and the cold, blustery Philadelphia climate wasn't aiding in the spread of the irritating common cold, which was indeed, still irritatingly common. Her and Peter never quite gelled with the rest of their peers musically, as they never nestled into the comfort of top forty pop music, but instead discovered a love for death metal and its adjacent genres. It fit both of their moods and past experiences, which gave them an outlet for their aggression. China had just begun their conquest, which at the time was referred to on the news as a "border skirmish", but Philadelphia had changed overnight. Chinatown began getting vandalized by scared and ignorant locals, who feared that the Chinese living among them were somehow involved or responsible for what was beginning to happen in Asia. Storefronts were vandalized with slurs and threats of violence, and people were attacked without reason, despite the victims not even being of Chinese descent. Fear, spurred on by the media machine which ran almost entirely on fear, did nothing to ease tensions for the local Chinese, and by ignorance, the local Koreans, Japanese, Vietnamese, and Thai.

Denise had grown scared of the city that she called home for her entire life. The irony hadn't been lost on her that she was a fifth generation Chinese American in the city of brotherly love.

She walked to work with her backpack slung over one shoulder. The streets felt different, despite looking the same as they always had, save for a few new signs here and there. She walked up to the door to her work - a restaurant now famous in Center City for its authentic Fujian cuisine, which was a rarity among the commonly seen Sichuan cuisine around the tri-state area of New Jersey, Delaware, and

Pennsylvania. She heard a friendly voice bellow from the kitchen, "Denise! You're here! Good, good, come back here! I have something for you to try!"

Mister Lin, the owner and head chef, was from Nanjing county in the southern part of Fujian province, and was always excited about adding new menu items. Denise breathed in the aromas coming from the kitchen and let out an ecstatic sigh. In the back of her mind, she thought about what she had seen on the news. She couldn't help but worry about what was happening in China. Fujian was one of the first provinces to declare autonomy from the People's Republic and as such established a healthy trade route with the United States. Mister Lin was overjoyed when he could get fresh ingredients from his old home to serve to his neighbors in his new home. Specifically, the dish that put his restaurant on the map, a creative take on Bak kut teh with noodles imparted with the flavor of red yeast rice and dressed with an oil infused with a Shaoxing wine reduction.

"Hurry, you have to try this! I think I'm really onto something!" he said with excitement in his voice. Denise picked up her pace and trotted back to the kitchen. She could smell the spices in the broth that had been simmering since the early morning, before the sun had risen. Mister Lin's smile greeted her warmly, and she returned a smile in turn. He hurried over to the dish he had just prepared and urged her to come over to it. She put her backpack down and brushed her long, dark hair over her shoulders so she could lean in and smell the dish.

"I made drunken ribs, marinated in Shaoxing wine, with a side of stir fried misua noodles. I took one of the ribs and shredded it and tossed it with the noodles. What do you think?"

Denise was delighted by the fragrance of the dish, and the simplicity of plating with the noodles acting as a bed for the ribs which were piled elegantly on top in an almost tripod fashion. She eagerly grabbed the top rib and took a small bite. The meat was tender and delicious, but still stuck to the bone with some rigidity. It was cooked to perfection. She let out sighs of satisfaction as the flavor coated her tongue.

"Try the noodles, the red yeast rice adds an earthy sweetness to them," Mister Lin said. He quickly handed her a pair of chopsticks, and she grabbed a pinch of noodles. They were evenly coated with sauce but not greasy. The vegetables were still crisp but cooked through, and the bits of tender drunken rib throughout them lent themselves beautifully to the texture and flavor of the entire dish.

"Wǒde mā ya!" she exclaimed. She was always surprised at how good the food was, even though she knew how talented he was as a chef.

"Do you like it?"

"Mister Lin, this is incredible!"

"Good! It's today's special. Go ahead and get changed and get ready for service. We're almost fully booked today, and you have to be hostess and waitress tonight!"

"I know, I know! You didn't forget about my concert, did you?"

"Of course not. My daughter will be here in a few hours. She'll take over for you when you're ready."

"Thank you so much mister Lin!"

He smiled as she grabbed her backpack and headed back into the bathroom to change. She put on an elegant outfit with a black, form fitting dress shirt and sleek, black slacks. She looked at herself in the mirror and noticed some of the sauce from the drunken ribs still remained near the corner of her mouth and promptly wiped it away. She washed her hands and face thoroughly, and then plopped a large, heavy bag full of makeup onto the sink. She carefully applied a bit of lipstick, paying special attention to the areas affected from trying mister Lin's meal, and headed out to the dining area to prepare. The restaurant held an early bird service after their lunch time got too crowded, and diners were eager to be able to get a seat. The benefit to this was that Denise got to start early, and as such would be out in time to go to her concert.

Her work day was just like any normal day. The diners were eager to eat as she hustled back and forth from the kitchen to the tables, and seated the new diners as they came in for their reservations. The sky eventually grew dark, and the bright lights of Chinatown illuminated the streets as the late-night diners came in for their meals. Once the clock read 7:30 in the evening, Denise was relieved that her shift was up, and once mister Lin's daughter stepped through the door, she grinned. She was finally free to see the concert she was looking forward to for so long with her good friend Peter. She rushed back to the bathroom to get changed. She put on a t-shirt with the almost illegible logo of a band she recently saw, followed by a denim jacket emblazoned with patches of other bands she endorsed. The jeans she had were taut, but ripped, and her boots went almost to her knees. She stepped out of the bathroom with confidence, but nevertheless stopped in the kitchen to say goodbye to mister Lin, who she loved like a father.

"I'm off to my show! Thanks again for letting me get out early. I can't thank you enough!"

Mister Lin looked over to her and smiled, while he still chopped the vegetables on his cutting board. She hurried out the door. As she left, she waved and smiled to mister Lin's daughter who had taken her spot at the front, welcoming guests in an elegant black outfit.

The venue was around the corner on 10th and Arch Streets. She was eager to get onto 10th so she could get right to the corner where the venue was and meet up with Peter. She ducked down a side street and picked up her pace. She had heard a boisterous conversation behind her but didn't pay it any mind. The conversation grew hushed, but remained close to her. She turned around to look, and saw only a blur approach her face as she was knocked to the ground.

She heard laughter as she came back to her senses, and saw a group of men around her, which had encircled her so she couldn't escape.

"Where are you off to? Gonna' start blowing us up now too?" one of the men said.

"I got something she can blow!" another one of the men laughed.

How pathetically cliché, she thought, *with everything going on right now in China you'd at least think they could be a little more creative.*

She placed her hand under her nose, which was beginning to crust over with blood. Before she could fully comprehend the situation she was in, the men ferociously grabbed her and began to tear at her clothes. *This can't be happening,* she thought with embarrassment, *not now. Is this how I die? A group of racist drunks? Fucking seriously?*

Her instinct was to fight back, her clutch had a stylish handle, which was fashioned to look like brass knuckles with three spikes protruding in between each rounded finger hole. With all of her might, she blindly swung at one of the men in front of her and gashed his forehead and eye, which began to bleed profusely.

"You fucking bitch!" he exclaimed, holding his face in agony.

Another one of the men, presumably his friend, wasn't pleased with her attempt at self-defense and began beating her violently. After an indeterminate number of blows, her ears began to ring with a loud, echoing screech. Another loud sound permeated the alley. Two of the men fell where they stood, and the rest scattered like cockroaches. She could have sworn she heard her name being cried out, but she swore she was imagining things until she saw mister Lin, who picked her up and held her.

"Denise, please tell me you're okay. Did they hurt you?" He frantically checked to see if she was okay as he removed his coat to cover her in the frigid January weather. "I'm going to call the police. Stay with me, okay? We're going to get you to a hospital."

Her eyes were heavy, and she longed for sleep more than anything, if only to escape the pain which buzzed through her face.

Almost a half an hour later, the police arrived with multiple ambulances. Mister Lin spoke to the police and explained what had happened. When asked how and why he was even in the alley, he told the police that she had forgotten her extra pay. He had set it aside for her to use at the concert she was going to. It was a bonus for taking on such a busy day by herself. She wanted to smile when she heard him, but her face was so swollen she could barely see, let alone speak.

Paramedics came and put her onto a gurney. They hauled her quickly towards the ambulance. Through her swollen eye, filled with tears and blood, she was able to make out a glimpse of mister Lin, who was in handcuffs, with a pistol on the ground next to him. She wanted to cry out. *He saved me*, she screamed in her mind. *He saved me from those monsters!* But she couldn't get the words out.

As she was loaded into the ambulance, she saw the two lifeless bodies of her assailants. The others had gotten away, but two of them weren't so lucky. She knew that mister Lin had a gun in the restaurant, and she was always nervous about it. At this very moment, she felt immense guilt for the fact that he was being taken into police custody for it.

The ambulance sped off to the hospital, and the loud siren hurt her ears, even from inside the vehicle. The paramedics affixed an oxygen mask to her face and began to try to clean the blood from her wounds. The drive to the hospital was a blur as she slipped in and out of consciousness. When she fully awoke, she was in a hospital bed, surrounded by nurses and a doctor. One of the nurses stepped away to fetch more gauze for her wounds, and she saw a man that didn't look like any doctor she had ever seen. He was clad in military garb from head to toe. He wore a distinguished hat which bore a regal insignia, and a coat decorated with countless awards and stripes. She had trouble hearing anything with the raucous movement of nurses, the beeps and shuffling of medical equipment, and the ringing that still remained in her ears.

"We'll have her transferred immediately, mister Schuck," she heard the doctor say.

Who is this man? What does he want with me? Transferred where? I'm already in a hospital! She thought in a panic.

"Nurse, if you would please. We're moving her to surgery," the doctor ordered coldly.

The military man left without a word, and after the nurse injected the liquid into her intravenous drip, she had no choice but to sleep.

In what felt like the blink of an eye, she woke up in a drastically different room. There were no windows, and only one doctor and one nurse.

"Where am I?" she uttered. Her voice was strained from the sedatives.

"You, my dear miss Huang, are about to make history, but don't worry yourself. You're in the care of some of the best doctors in the country," the man grinned an evil, malicious grin.

"Doctor, begin the preparations. Our specialists will be here shortly. You need only prepare miss Huang for the procedure."

The doctor looked over at the nurse and gave a subtle head nod, and once again, Denise fell into sleep.

Her body was paralyzed, yet she could hear and understand what was going on around her.

"Bring over the laparascope. We're going to begin with the hysterectomy. Once that is complete, we'll move onto the bilateral salpingectomy-oophorectomy. He was very clear that the entire procedure must be completed, and then their medical team will take over the rest."

She wanted to scream, but couldn't move.

Hours went by, and she felt the prodding, carving, and pulling happening inside of her body. Her urge to cry, and inability to do so, caused her immense dread and rage. She finally surrendered to the anger and pain when new voices entered the room.

"Is the procedure complete, doctor?"

"Yes sir, full hysterectomy and bilateral salpingectomy-oophorectomy."

"Good, we can get started. Thank you for your help doctor, nurse. You can return to your duties."

"If there's anything el-"

"We'll take it from here, doctor. If you would, please."

More hours passed in agony. She had to feel every sensation, every push, prod, and cut.

They've put something inside of me, her voice screamed in her head, *what are they doing to me?!*

Time continued to flow, as did the pain, until eventually, she awoke. She feigned sleep so as not to alert those in the room to her consciousness.

"Is the procedure complete?"

"Yes sir."

"How is she responding to it?"

"I don't want to be overly optimistic or celebratory, sir, but from what we can tell, she has completed the procedure one hundred percent successfully. The gene has synchronized beautifully with her own, and we should be able to see the fruits of our labor within a few days."

"Very good. I need to get in contact with Wilkins."

"Sir?"

"She's going to Petty Island."

"Sir, she still needs time to rest, if we try to transport her now it may cause her more damage while her tissues are synchronizing and adapting to the new gene."

"You said so yourself that the procedure was, and I quote, a one hundred percent success, correct? Do you doubt your work?"

"Well, no sir, but-"

"Then she's going to Petty Island."

She heard a distinct beep.

"Commander Wilkins, I have good news. Project Manticore has been a success, and the subject will be at the Petty Island facility within the hour for further examination and preliminary studies."

What she heard next deafened her in the same way she was deafened in the alleyway. The ringing returned, and as much as she tried to continue to feign her sleep, she couldn't help but jump when the loud bangs assaulted her ears. The doctor and nurse fell limp to the floor.

"This facility is to be wiped clean. Do you understand?"

"Yes sir." A previously unknown voice confirmed.

The man in decorated garb walked over to her, and her fear intensified greatly as her heart began to pound out of her chest.

"You, my dear miss Huang, you are going to make history. Don't be afraid. You're in the care of some of the best scientists in the world."

***

"Hey Joey, I think she's awake," Miller said, his voice distant.

"Welcome back. You were out damn near an entire day. Are you okay? You were talking in your sleep. Mostly gibberish, but it didn't seem like you were resting too easy," Marquez said to the girl, whose vision was still foggy from being freshly roused from her dream.

"Joey..." She uttered under her breath.

"Shit, we haven't introduced ourselves properly yet. I'm Joe, Joe Marquez. That there's Henry Miller," he said, pointing over to Miller who was inspecting his rifle, "and the guy smoking over there is Phil Waters."

Her eyes darted to each of them, until her gaze locked onto a small pile of stones with scraps of armor and a helmet on top. She fought back tears, and sniffled, as she knew who it was, though she didn't know his name.

"That... that was Andrew Feig. Look, none of that was your fault, okay? We're all pretty fucked up about it... they planted a bomb in his chest for Christ's sake. How were you supposed to know that we weren't your enemy?" Marquez said somberly. He placed a hand on her shoulder.

"Denise," She said, with a lump in her throat, "My name is Denise."

"It's a pleasure to meet you, Denise. We've been taking turns sleeping, in shifts, to make sure Schuck hasn't sent anyone down to, you know, take us out."

Her eyes widened, and she sprang up from her seated position.

"Schuck," She uttered his name with a dry rage.

"You know him?" Marquez asked.

"Of fuckin' course she does, he brought her here, I'm sure she had to have heard his name at some point. Probably from any number of the other sorry bastards he sent down here to their deaths," Waters chimed in as he took a drag from his cigarette.

"He's the one that did this to me... he turned me into this."

"What do you mean? He told us you were some sort of bio weapon developed by the Chinese government, that they captured you during the war," Marquez looked extremely puzzled.

"I'm from Philly. I work... worked... at a restaurant in Chinatown."

"Are you fuckin' kidding me? She's local?! I told you! I told you all that those pieces of shit were lying to us from the get go," Waters said as he began to pace. He was getting visibly angry.

"Are you all-" she began to ask.

"Yeah, we're local too. Jersey and PA. All ex-military," Marquez tried to answer the obvious questions.

"As if we had a choice to be anything but after they started fuckin' mandatory service," Waters added.

"Mandatory service? What do you mean?" Denise asked. She looked markedly confused.

"You know... mandatory service in the military... for the war effort? China basically conquered their way across Asia and Europe, remember?" Waters replied.

"I thought it was a... a 'border skirmish'. They talked about it on the news, but the president said he

198

was going to send aid. The United Nations were going to put a stop to it, I..."

"How long have they fuckin' held you here?" Waters said. The stubby cigarette hung off his lip, and the wisps of smoke caused his eyes to water.

Denise stared at the floor, confused.

"Have you heard of Rose Cross? It's a military base in Philly, right along the Delaware," Miller asked.

"Of course... they raised the small business tax to almost twenty percent to build it, mister Lin was pissed. It was nearly halfway done before they... took me."

"Jesus fuckin' Christ. What year do you think it is?" Waters asked. He knew the answer wasn't going to be correct.

"2140?" Denise replied, knowing her answer wasn't going to be correct.

"Okay, look, Denise? This isn't going to be easy, but-" Marquez tried to soften the blow.

"Just tell me what year it is," she grabbed him by the collar of his armor.

"It's 2145," Marquez said and averted his eyes.

"What happened while I was here? What did I miss?!" Denise said in a panic.

"Well, if the last thing you remember is 2140, you were correct in that Rose Cross was about half way complete. It was one of many that were being built across the country. You might also remember that at this point, the Chinese military had already made its way over to northern Kazakhstan and parts of Russia and Ukraine."

"Yeah, and the U.N. said they were sending aid to those regions and anyone else affected! They were going to stop the conflict! What the fuck happened?"

"The president backed out of sending aid. He said there were too many problems to deal with domestically. In reality, he was just preparing for a larger conflict, and truthfully, purposefully dragging it out. Once the U.S. pulled out, other members of the U.N. pulled out too. In the summer of 2040, the United States enacted two years of mandatory military service, emergency order. That's when we all got pulled in to go to training. By 2141, there were Chinese troops as far as Germany and Italy, with a clear course towards Britain."

"So, what, nobody did anything? Nobody fought back?"

"Every country they entered fought back, but they didn't do so with any kind of real success. Iran was able to hold them off long enough for the Chinese government to shift their focus towards moving northwest, but otherwise, they went almost entirely uncontested."

"What happened was, the United States, which is now the 'Democratic Republic of the Americas', fuckin' stupid ass name, was waiting on purpose, like Joey said. They sat on their fuckin' asses to take advantage of the political opportunity that the war presented. The U.S. government didn't fully intervene until towards the end of 2141. To make a long story short, it fuckin' crippled the economy. Not just here, but also in Canada, all of South America, and every single country in Europe and Asia that the war touched. The U.S. knew this would happen and took advantage of it. For two years, they sent people like us to the front lines to get mowed down like cattle. Me and Feig were in the artillery regiment. Marquez and Miller were fuckin' meat shields. We ended up routing the primary Chinese units around London, and that was when China finally surrendered. The president used the propaganda from the war - the United States being the saviors of the world - to take full economic and political control of South America, with Canada soon to follow suit..." Waters trembled as he spoke. His rage grew after every sentence.

"Five years..." Denise said under her breath.

"Feds took control of everything. Hospitals, grocery stores, manufacturers, shipping, everything under the fuckin' sun. Not hard to imagine what happened next," Waters raised his fingers to count each as he spoke, until eventually he threw his hand into the air

"I've been trapped here for five... years..." Denise said, her voice trembling.

"Hey, hey, look just take it easy. I know it's a lot to take in, but..." Marquez wanted to console her, but he knew his words fell on deaf ears.

"I was attacked in an alleyway by a group of drunks. After the news was spreading about China, things got bad in the city. I was on my way to a... a concert. I heard voices behind me, and when I turned around, they hit me in the face and knocked me down."

"For fucks sake…" Waters said with disgust.

"I fell to the ground… they called me names and started ripping my clothes off. I… I hit one of them with my purse, my, uh, my clutch. It had a handle shaped like brass knuckles. I thought it was cool, so…"

Marquez shook his head, repulsed at what he was imagining came next, "You don't have to-"

"No, it's fine. It's fine. He was bleeding, badly, and his friend started punching me in the face. I blacked out… and then I heard two gunshots. My boss, mister Lin… he ran out to follow me because I," she chuckled slightly, "I left some extra cash he set aside for me. We were understaffed and overbooked, and I ran the service myself for almost an entire day. I always gave him shit about that gun, and then he saved my life…"

"Denise… I'm sorry," Marquez said awkwardly.

"You didn't do it, so what are you sorry for? Anyway I- I got put onto a gurney, they loaded me into an ambulance, and mister Lin got arrested. At the hospital, the doctors and nurses were buzzing around me like flies. I saw a man dressed up in a military outfit, stiff as a board, talking to the doctor. He had me transferred to a surgery room. They…" She began to weep.

None of the other prisoners said a word.

"They," she sniffled, "I think they removed my uterus… and they put something in its place. The man… Schuck. He said I was going to make history, and when I woke up, I was in a cage. Here."

Waters yelled out in anger, and punched the wall nearest him fiercely.

"I'm so... so sorry about your friend, I just, I didn't-" Denise's voice petered out as the lump in her throat grew larger.

"You've got nothing to fuckin' apologize for... you weren't told a damned thing. Neither were we. I'm sorry to you though," Waters paused, walked over to Denise, and took her hands in his. He hung his head and stared at his feet. "I'm sorry that I wanted to kill you and just be done with this place. I'm sorry that I doubted Marquez when he swore up and down that you were actually... a person. I'm sorry that... after you killed Feig... I almost killed you in your sleep," Denise opened her mouth to begin to speak. "No, please, just... just listen." Waters lifted his head and locked his eyes with hers. "I'm sorry for everything. I don't believe in killing innocent people... We were all lied to in some sick fuckin' game, and right now, I only believe in killing monsters. Killing the degenerate fucks that dragged us here. Okay?"

Denise nodded and wiped her nose.

"Now listen, Schuck and his pals have the same ammunition we do. This shit has been engineered specifically to weaken Denise in her other form, but as I was digging through the corpses of the other fire team looking for Feig's helmet, I noticed something. This neurotoxin she has is powerful shit. One of the poor fucks we shot in the face doesn't have much left of a head anymore. The toxin basically, I guess you could say it ate most of it. The good news is, we can use that against them. The bad news is, they can use it

203

against us, and they've got numbers," Waters shifted to a serious tone in an instant.

"The other problem... I mean, I don't know about you guys, but I'm starving," Miller said.

"Yeah... We can't wait here forever. They could, if they really wanted to, just starve us out. We can't wait this out. We have to do something," Marquez said as he placed a hand on his grumbling stomach.

"Well first, can we at least get Denise some fuckin' clothes? There's about a dozen dudes around the corner that aren't going to be needing theirs any time soon," Waters blushed uncharacteristically.

"Guys, turn around. Denise, do you want to go get dressed?" Marquez asked while placing his hand up to avert his eyes from her exposed skin.

She said nothing, and walked around the corner to remove the armor from one of the dead soldiers and get dressed.

"Grab a gun while you're at it," Waters hollered while still turned around.

"I've... never used a gun before..." Denise said, shyly from around the corner as she pulled the armor, riddled with bullet holes over her head.

"Don't worry about that," Waters said, still hiding. "We'll show you."

Chapter 10 - Mantichora Foederaterum

The silence was deafening. It was Marquez's turn on watch, and the lack of sound was simultaneously comforting and foreboding. The comfort came from the fact that Schuck's men weren't presently an immediate threat. They were alone in an abandoned office, connected to abandoned hallways that led to even more abandoned rooms. The oppressive quietness extended to the island itself. For well over a day now, none of the prisoners had heard so much as a footstep or the whirr of a vehicle overhead. The foreboding came from the fact that he knew that the silence could be broken at any moment. Schuck's men had at least six known points of entry, and the thought in the back of everyone's mind was that Schuck didn't necessarily need to use a point of entry. For every second of calm due to the silence, there was an equally nervous second at the potential it represented.

Marquez heard a shuffle coming from behind him and turned around quickly while his hands clutched his rifle into his shoulder.

"Shit! You scared me. I thought you were asleep," he said in an angry but hushed tone. His heart pounded with anxiety.

"I'm sorry. I feel like I've slept enough lately. I keep having that same dream, and I'd just... I'd rather not keep reliving it," Denise said with tired eyes.

"I understand that more than you'd believe..." Marquez said with a small smile. "Are you ready for some weapons training?"

"I've never even held a gun before. I'm nervous," Denise responded frankly.

"You've got nothing to be nervous about, I'm going to give you a crash course. Before we get into how everything actually works, there are a few principles that you always have to adhere to. They're going to sound obvious, and maybe a little dumb, but trust me. It's important."

Denise looked slightly puzzled, but Marquez figured she was still groggy from having recently woken up.

"Number one, you always treat a weapon as if it's loaded. Even if you know with absolute certainty that there's no magazine in it and there's no round in the chamber - you treat it as if it's loaded, okay?"

Denise nodded.

"Number two, don't point it at anything you don't intend to destroy. This one is especially important when you factor in number one. Pretend that there's a laser extending from the barrel that kills anything it touches. That's why we're always aiming ours at the ground."

There was a brief moment of silence.

"Number three, keep your finger off of the trigger, outside of the trigger guard, until your sights are on your target and you intend to fire."

Denise nodded once more.

"Finally, number four. Be one hundred percent certain of your target and what's behind it. If you take out one of Schuck's men but take a chunk out of my neck in the process, I'm going to be pissed, okay?"

Denise smiled to stifle a laugh and nodded.

"So, what are the four rules?"

"Always act as if it's loaded, don't aim at anything you don't want to destroy, keep your finger off the trigger until you know what you're shooting, and know what you're shooting and what's behind it," Denise said with confidence and clarity.

"Damn, I was at least expecting you to get them in the wrong order or something. You're a fast learner, which is good, because now we're going to go over how it works."

Marquez released the magazine from his rifle and pulled the charging handle back, which ejected the round from the chamber. He held it up so she could see as best she could into the chamber to confirm that it was empty. He explained what each part of the rifle was and what it did, and she listened intently. She knew it could be her only way out of this prison. Many minutes went by as she took mental notes of each action and what order to perform them in.

"How does the, um, the bolt stay back once it runs out of bullets?" she asked shyly.

"That's a great question. Remember the bolt catch I showed you earlier? The magazine has a follower which not only guides the cartridges into the chamber, but after firing the last round, the follower engages the bolt catch and, well, catches the bolt.

That way you can quickly reload without having to pull the charging handle again, you just hit your bolt release like I showed you and you're back in action."

"I had no idea they were so complicated," Denise said with surprised.

"They're just like any other machine, it's complicated until you get a feel for it, but ultimately it comes down to experience and repetition. You weren't a great driver when you first started right? Who am I kidding, you're from Philly, you were never destined to be a great driver," Marquez chuckled heartily.

"You know I have a gun, and now I actually know how to use it, right?" Denise said with a scowl, which quickly transformed into a smirk.

For the next half hour or so, Marquez helped her with aiming and stance, making sure she opened the correct eye and placed the stock in the correct position.

"When you're aiming you want to bring the weapon up to your cheek, not your cheek to the weapon. Just bring your shoulder up and it'll bring the stock with it. That way you're not craning your neck, see? Like this," Marquez demonstrated, and Denise followed suit perfectly.

She spent hours disassembling the rifle and reassembling it. Marquez eventually went to sleep and Waters took over watch. Denise continued practicing. Waters watched, impressed, and smoked a short of a cigarette he had the night before.

"If I didn't know any better, I'd think you were an experienced shooter," Waters said as the ash flung from his mouth.

Denise looked over at Waters and while maintaining eye contact pulled the charging handle, pressed the bolt release, placed her left hand back on the forward grip in mere seconds. Waters smiled a wide, tight grin, making sure the cigarette didn't fall out of his lips.

A sound like static hummed throughout the corridors and rooms. Miller and Marquez woke up and hurried over to Waters and Denise.

"What's that sound?" Miller said groggily.

"Rain," Waters said looking up at the ceiling as if it were the sky.

The rain pattering sounded hollow, like on the roof of a car, and was a welcome relief from the painful silence.

"I know none of you want to talk about it, but let's just cut the bullshit here, okay? We have no food or water, and we're on day two, I think, of being stuck down here without either. We need a plan to get out of here, and we need to understand that this isn't going to be some spy movie shit. There's going to be resistance. Lots of it," Waters said directly.

"What's the point?" Miller shook off his grogginess quickly, and began getting more animated. "There's four of us and Christ knows how many of them. Face it, we're fucking dead."

"Small groups of men have taken on larger groups successfully countless times throughout history. The

American revolution and The Winter War to name a few. Do you know anything about The Winter War?" Waters asked rhetorically. "You see, Soviet Russia invaded Finland shortly after the second World War kicked off. The Finnish state at the time was tiny by comparison, and barely kept much of an army. Basically, a bunch of reservists and a handful of artillery. The Russians sent over 800,000 troops, but they were caught by surprise, and do you know how?" Waters asked again rhetorically. "The Finns, despite their drastically smaller army, knew how to work in small groups, and they used the heavily wooded geography to their advantage. The Soviets, much like Schuck and friends, were used to more... traditional combat, on open fields and urban settings."

Miller's head drooped down and Waters continued.

"So, despite having manpower and firepower, the Soviets didn't count on the Finns being so crafty. They picked off Russian tanks, supply convoys, blocked roads, and controlled the entire conflict in countless engagements," Waters finished.

"Yeah but didn't they still lose the war? They signed the Moscow Peace Treaty and gave up a bunch of their land," Denise chimed in.

"I'll be damned. Who taught you history? You sure as shit didn't learn that at school," Waters questioned.

"My father used to watch old war documentary vids. We only had one screen in the house, so I watched them too."

"Well, you're correct. Finland gave up almost all of Karelia, but to your point, I doubt Schuck and Wilkins are going to be drawing up a fuckin' peace treaty for us anytime soon."

Miller perked his head up to speak, but Waters cut him off, as he knew that it was going to be another defeatist quip. "My point is, we're going to have to use guerilla tactics. Hit and run. Considering you two were in London, I expected you to understand that out of the gate, Miller, but I'm not trying to shit on you, okay? The artillery unit got hit hard by guerillas, so believe me when I say that I know what works."

"First order of business is to understand what we're up against. They've got at least fifty men that we know of, and who knows how many in the main complex. The walls are lined with turrets that'll rip us to shreds if we get anywhere near the walls," Marquez took on a serious tone.

"I know that all too well... Look," Denise lifted the armor she was wearing to show the left side of her ribs where multiple large scars resided.

"Jesus Christ," Waters said in disbelief. Denise then turned around and showed the scar on her back where the bullets exited. "How the fuck did you survive that?"

"When I'm... you know, that thing, I can heal really quickly if I'm hurt, but I don't exactly come out unscathed. These scars were the first ones I got by my own actions. I thought I could climb the wall and get out. Obviously, that didn't work out too well. The rest are from the others that came down here...:" Denise lowered her eyes.

"So obviously, gunning right for the walls isn't going to work. We'll be dead before we even reach them," Waters said, and crossed his arms. "Ideally, we're going to want to stick to places with decent cover, and places we're familiar with. Both would be best, but we can't be particularly choosy either."

"We have no food or water," Miller said, groaning.

"Which brings me to my next point. Escaping the sub level is the first priority. The second is making our way to somewhere we can get food, water, and any other useful supplies."

"What about the mess hall?" Marquez asked, looking at Waters inquisitively.

"Mess hall is too obvious, and likely to be stacked with guards. Familiar, sure, but not much in the way of cover."

Marquez stroked his chin in deep thought. Miller began to pace, while Waters crouched down and stared at the ground. Denise felt useless because her knowledge of the facility was limited to where they were currently stuck.

"What about the medical bay? The food may be limited, but they've got to have something there, and plus we can get some medical supplies while we're there," Miller said with a smirk of satisfaction on his face. "We were able to sneak in there to see Feig, and-"

"And by now the entrances are also probably fuckin' stacked," Waters cut him off.

"Yeah, but remember the shaft in the maintenance tunnels? It goes to the generator room. We'd just have to clear the shit blocking the way!" Miller began to get more animated.

"And we decided to not use that way because who the fuck wants to move a bunch of rocks? It'd take hours," Waters said, growing increasingly agitated.

"I can move them," Denise said, as the other prisoners stared at her in disbelief.

"Of course. We've got the fucking Manticore!" Miller laughed.

"Wait, wait, hold on. The maintenance tunnels are a tight space, how do we know she can even-" Marquez couldn't help but try to be a voice of reason, but was cut off.

"I can fit. I've hidden there before. From them... and from you."

"Won't it be loud if you go clawing through a pile of rocks?" Waters questioned.

"I'm still able to control myself when I'm... like that. I can move them enough so that we can get through. That way it won't take too long, and it won't be too loud either."

"And that will give us a straight shot to the medical bay! See?" Miller threw his hands up.

"Yeah, but you'll also remember, I said there was no guarantee that they didn't weld that hatch shut after they annexed off the sub level. We'd just be clearing one obstacle to get to another."

Miller scrunched his face to express something like a combination of surprise and exasperation, and quickly gestured his hands towards Denise. Waters looked at Marquez, who gritted his teeth and shrugged.

"I can tear the door open if I need to. That will be pretty loud though," Denise said candidly.

"But we'll be in the generator room, we could cut the fucking power right then and there! We've got night vision, thermals, anything we need in our helmets," Miller was champing at the bit, as he had a strong gut feeling that his solution was the best one. There was also a part of him that simply wanted to be right and for Waters to admit it.

"They have the same gear we have and then some... but it would level the playing field a bit. Might also cause some confusion, which we can use to our advantage..."

"Oh, we've got more than what we came down here with, Waters," Miller walked over to the hallway filled with corpses of the soldiers that had attacked them days ago. "Look at this. Smoke grenades, flash bangs... ammo, sidearms, this guy's got an incendiary! Never mind all of this extra ammo. Plus, they probably have a newer recipe of the special shit they gave us." Miller's voice was slightly muffled from speaking around the corner from the other prisoners.

"He's got a point. This plan just might work, and we've got plenty of extra firepower. The fact that they brought all of this extra shit down means they must see us as a threat," Marquez said.

"Yeah, and her."

"Well, of course, but..." Marquez trailed off.

"There's another small problem that you guys seem to be forgetting. Every time Denise changes shape, she's going to obliterate whatever armor she's wearing and be back down to her birthday suit," Waters said somberly. He didn't want to blow any more holes in the plan, but knew it had to be brought up. Miller walked back around the corner with his hands full of explosives and ammunition magazines.

"Shit... this is true..." Marquez said, defeated.

"I'll just... take off the armor, move the rocks, and then put it back on when I'm done. It's not like it's anything you haven't seen before, and I think I'm a little bit more concerned about not dying than you staring at my tits for a few minutes." The other prisoners blushed.

"I didn't mean to - fuck, look, I'm sorry. I just, does it hurt to change back and forth? Christ we could stay down here for a fuckin' week playing twenty questions and I'd still be lost about this whole thing, I just..." Waters stammered.

"It hurts, but I'm kind of used to it. It's not pleasant, but... I can deal with it. I'm sorry too, you know, you're just trying to be thorough, I just... we're-"

"We're in a moldy hallway, underground, surrounded by corpses, trying to come up with a plan to take on fifty or so soldiers by ourselves, if we're lucky, and somehow get out of here alive. Fuckin' lunatics, I know..."

"So that's it?" Miller said excitedly. "This is the plan?"

"I guess so," Marquez said. "Let's just go over everything from the top and make sure we have everything in order."

***

The prisoners sat in a circle on the damp, musty floor. Waters scrounged up another pack of cigarettes from one of the dead soldiers in the hallway. As the ember hanging from his lips flailed, he gave an animated and passionate rundown of their plan, which was to be set in motion a mere few hours from then. Miller recited the plan practically word for word, reassuring everyone that he was paying attention. Marquez gave his version, which was fundamentally similar, and finally, Denise followed suit to ensure that everyone was on the same page.

Waters pulled out another cigarette and passed the pack around the circle.

"Come on ladies and gentlemen, I normally wouldn't resort to peer pressure, but there's a very good chance we could all die tomorrow," Waters said with a smirk.

Denise reluctantly pulled a cigarette out and pressed it between her lips. Marquez had just finished lighting his and reached over with a cupped hand and lit her cigarette. She breathed in deeply and exhaled the smoke through her nostrils. She threw her head back and let out a deep sigh.

"I quit these damned things after two years," She took another drag. "Way too expensive, and I got sick of coughing all the time, but right now... this might sound strange, I finally feel human again, you know?"

Waters laughed. "Leave it to humanity to need a vice to feel alive. I'm sure as shit guilty as charged. What are we if we're not allowed to fail? I shudder to think what my wife would have thought of me if I wasn't able to fuck up every now and again. Learn a little. Get my heart broken a few times, break a few of my own, drink way too much, all that shit."

"The only mistake I was allowed to make was taking a shortcut to a concert venue..." Denise said while flicking the ash from the end of her cigarette.

"With any luck, come tomorrow, we'll be off of this damn island and you'll be able to make a few more. On your own terms this time," Waters looked into her eyes and spoke with a gentle, fatherly voice.

"We doing our last words now? Just in case?" Miller said with a chuckle.

"You watch too many movies, Miller," Marquez said, giving Miller a nudge in the shoulder.

"I'm serious though, man. I mean, we don't know what's going to happen. We're probably going to get shot to fucking pieces, so this could be our last chance to get anything off our chests, you know?"

"Fine, fine. Miller, I have to tell you... I always was fond of your mother. She made eyes at me the one year at Thanksgiving, and I-"

"Fuck you, Joey! Asshole, I'm serious!" Miller was sure that they couldn't hear him, as Waters had burst out into a hearty laugh. Even Denise was laughing, though he couldn't be sure if she was just nervous or actually laughing at him, so he decided to focus his anger at Marquez and Waters. "Look, all I'm saying is that if there's anything bothering you, now's the time to say it, even if we're all going to get smoked tomorrow."

The laughter died down, and the prisoners sat in silence for a few moments, taking in the unavoidable truth in Miller's sentiment. Waters put his cigarette out and rested his chin on his hands.

"I, uh... I feel personally responsible for Feig's death. I fuckin' knew they were up to some shady shit when we were in the med bay. I knew something was wrong, but I kept it to myself. Something tells me he had a feeling too, but that bastard was always too pragmatic for his own good. Never wanted to bother anyone... always wanted to fix it himself."

"Phil..." Marquez didn't know what else to say.

"It's alright, don't worry about me. He was a fixer, man. Guy could fix fuckin' anything. Christ, I remember years ago, before the war started, he bought some vintage car from some old head."

"How vintage are we talking?" Miller said with excitement.

"Late 2040's, pretty much right before cars became mandatory electric."

"Holy shit, that thing must have been a dinosaur!"

"Tell me about it, hard to come by too. Body was rusted to shit, engine needed to be fully rebuilt from just sitting in some old fuck's garage for who knows how long. I gave him shit for spending so much on it, but he just did his thing. He gave me that little half-assed smirk he did, and started work on it immediately. Patched the body up in a few days. Still looked like shit because it needed paint, but I'm talking about extensive fuckin' damage that, to me, was beyond repair. Another week goes by, and I stop by the shop to see if he gave up yet. He's balls deep in the engine, and I ask him 'taking it out to fix that piece of shit?' and without even turning back he tells me he's putting it *back in* because he finished the fuckin' rebuild! Bent piston in cylinder three. The crazy son of a bitch found the specs and milled one out himself. He cleaned the sludgy build up off the cylinder walls, and Christ knows where he found the electronics for it, but he did. In two weeks, he rebuilt that car from the ground up. Painted it, started it right in front of me. I had to know how much it was worth, so I asked, and he just smiled and walked away."

"So how much was it worth?" Marquez asked.

"Son of a bitch never told me, and shortly after that they banned internal combustion vehicles. Everybody had to take the short-range hover cabs to get anywhere. Government seized it for scrap to serve the war effort shortly before we got drafted. Un-fuckin'-believable."

"Shit, I remember that ban going through. Everybody got their cars seized. I still hate those cabs. Is it just me or did they never feel safe?" Miller added.

"It ain't just you. Those things were fuckin' death traps. It's why they still hauled our asses over here by boat," Waters let out a small laugh, and his face once again turned towards the ground. "He was a fixer.

Even tried to fix me. Lost fuckin' cause, as I'm sure you all know by now. Denise maybe you not so much, but I'm sure you get a pretty clear picture by now. I blame myself for his death, and I'd trade places with him right now if I could. Best thing I can do though, is try to fix this fuckin' mess we're in. There. There's my peace."

The prisoners sat in awkward silence for a bit and eventually began to drift into sleep. Miller dropped first, snoozing away on a pile of cloth scrounged up from the surrounding area. Waters followed suit, snoring lightly on his back. Marquez and Denise layed on the floor in silence, hoping to fall asleep. An hour or so went by, and Denise tossed and turned, unable to get comfortable. She sat up and rested her elbows on her knees, placing her forehead on her interlocked fingers.

"Can't sleep?" Marquez whispered.

"I'm starving, and I'm thirsty, and I'm going to get killed soon," Denise whispered back.

"I know the situation we're in-I, I know it's not ideal, and you might even be entirely correct, but... if we do this, and we make it out of here, everything will be different."

"It already is different. The world I know of only exists in the past. I have no idea what the world looks like now. I don't even know what I look like now."

"You want to take a walk or something? Clear your head a little? I don't sleep well as it is, let alone the night before something like this... you know, suicide by armed forces."

Denise gave Marquez an angry look for his morbid joke, but nodded nonetheless to the prospect of a little jaunt in the musty hallways.

The two of them gingerly walked about, making sure not to make any noise that would alarm their fellow sleeping prisoners.

"I have this dream, well, it's a nightmare actually, almost every night. It's not always, but almost always. There was a girl down an alleyway in Knightsbridge. That's where me and Miller were stationed, front and center of the final push. I saw this girl, and there were soldiers around her, I wanted to protect her, you know?"

"Why are you telling me this?" Denise said, puzzled.

"That's a fair question. Well, Miller already knows this story, he was there. Not like, there with me, but our whole unit was in that region, and I had to make an official report and all that. Waters... Waters went through his own shit, and I didn't want to bother him with my gripes."

"So you're bothering me with your gripes?" she replied with a smirk.

"You're an unbiased third party. I can get it off my chest, and if you don't give two shits about it, then there's no harm done."

She looked off into the darkness for a moment and paused.

"So, you're in London, and there are soldiers surrounding a girl, and?"

"And they're... you know, they're not surrounding her for protection, they're scum."

"I know the type," She replied curtly.

"Shit, sorry, I didn't mean to-"

"No, it's okay. Really. Continue."

"So, they didn't see me yet, and I had the advantage. I killed all three of them. The one piece of shit still had his pants around his ankles."

"You saved her, right? That's a good thing."

"No... you see the one guy, his sidearm fell to the ground, and the girl, I don't fucking know what she thought, if it was shock, or if she truly believed I was the enemy even though I had just saved her life... I don't know, but she picked up the gun. I begged her not to raise it, I fucking begged her."

"Do you think you did the right thing?"

"I put a fucking bullet between her eyes. How is that the right thing?"

"If you didn't kill her attackers, would you have felt better knowing that you left her there to be raped to death?"

"Of course not!"

"Then out of confusion or not, she would have killed you, and even though she's dead, she got a better death than what she would have gotten at the hands of those men."

Marquez held back tears of rage and grief, striking the wall with the butt of his fist. Denise placed her hand gently on his shoulder.

"If she killed you, then chances are I wouldn't even have the chance of escaping this place. None of us would."

Marquez didn't respond.

"We've all done terrible things. Sometimes at the behest of other people. Sometimes because we didn't know any better. I killed innocent people dressed up as my enemy. You saw me, the real me, and you could have taken the easy way out and just killed me, but you didn't."

"Even if we killed you, they'd have just killed us after we were done. They wouldn't risk their secret getting out, and it sure as fuck wouldn't be the first time that they've killed someone to keep them quiet," Marquez said through a trembling voice.

"You saw that I was a person, and you didn't want to kill me. I don't think it's just the girl that's bothering you at this point... it's everyone. You were in a war... you were there against your will, and you had to make decisions that got people killed every single day of it... and now you have to kill again. Now we all have to kill again."

"I'm tired of it. I'm so fucking tired of it," Marquez wept and collapsed to the floor, burying his face in his hands.

Denise crouched down next to him and brought his head onto her shoulder.

"It's not going to stop. Waters and Feig were right," Marquez said muffled through his hands.

"What do you mean?"

"War, oppression, famine... It's not *the people* who start wars, it's the people in charge trying to win an election. They send kids who think they're fighting for their country to go kill kids who think they're fighting for theirs. Our government bombed hospitals during the war. Hospitals that were treating men and women from both sides of the conflict. They fucking killed their own people for a strategic advantage. They killed nurses and doctors. It doesn't matter to them, and it never will."

Denise was shocked but didn't say a word. She thought deeply about her own situation and the circumstances around it. *Why did they do what they did to me? Was I a random choice? Was I a chosen candidate? No, they just took me opportunistically from the hospital. Which one is worse? Are they the same? Does it matter whether it was planned or not? Are there more girls like me?* Her mind raced as she consoled Marquez who was now significantly calmer.

Marquez freed himself gently from her arm, and without looking over said through swollen puffy eyes, "Thank you. I'm sorry."

"Don't apologize. Thank you, too," she responded warmly. "Let's go get some sleep, I finally feel like I can."

"Me too."

The pair quietly made their way back to where their allies were still sleeping and did what they could to get comfortable. Within a few minutes, all four of the prisoners were firmly in a state of rest.

The hours went by, and eventually, the sun began to set behind the horizon. The darkness of the forest on the island began to deepen. The search lights throughout the Philadelphia skyline became starkly contrasted as the sun's light faded away. Petty Island remained eerily quiet. Completely still.

***

"Just as war is the natural consequence of monopoly, peace is the natural consequence of liberty."
— Gustave de Molinari

Chapter 11 - Love Like Blood

"Hey, Joey! Come on man, tonight's the night," Waters roughly jostled Marquez awake, "I don't know about you, but I'm fuckin' hungry, and if eating doesn't end up happening today, at least I can take a bullet to the head so I won't be hungry anymore, am I right?"

Miller was already upright and fully dressed in his armor and was pensively inspecting his weapon. Denise looked over at Marquez, and then back over to the helmet in her hands. She reluctantly placed the helmet onto her head and pressed firmly on the top to slide it down. Her hair bunched up under the helmet, much to her dismay.

Waters walked over to her and gestured for her to take the helmet off. "These things are shit for anyone with long hair, as you've now experienced first-hand. Here, pull your hair back in a loose ponytail."

Denise grabbed her hair and bunched it up as best she could in the armor that was oddly sized, as it had been pieced together with the most intact segments from the corpses in the hallway. Waters gently rocked the helmet from side to side over her head until it slid down to where her hands were holding her hair.

"You can let go now. This should keep it from getting in the way," he said, gently pushing the helmet down the rest of the way. "I know the whole kit doesn't fit perfectly, but it's the best of the bunch."

"Thank you," She replied shyly. She turned around, bent down, and grabbed her rifle. She began stuffing magazines into slots on her armor. She took one and slammed it into the magazine well. With a quick tap of the bottom, she brought her hand up to the charging handle and pulled it back with confidence. The bolt carrier group slammed forward with a loud metallic clang.

"Shit, you look better than fuckin' Miller does with that thing. Whoever taught you must be handsome *and* intelligent!" Waters said with a laugh.

Miller didn't take the bait, but it was too late to feign apathy - Waters had already seen him smirking in his helmet.

Marquez hurried to get his gear on and began arming up with whatever he could get his hands on. Miller and Waters had prudently gathered the weapons, magazines, and explosives from the corpses of the team from before and laid them out in an organized manner.

"Take whatever you can carry without it becoming a problem, that goes for every single one of us, alright?" Waters said with a serious tone.

"Should we go over the plan one more time, just to make sure?" Miller said with a hint of worry in his voice.

"Simple. We're going to take the maintenance tunnels until we reach the rubble. Denise is going to have to disrobe to be able to transform without ripping her armor to shreds. We turn around like gentlemen while she does the deed, quietly, and grants us passage to the maintenance hatch to the generator room of the medical bay," Waters said bluntly.

"Yeah but-" Miller tried to interject.

"-but, as we know, there's a chance that the hatch has been sealed shut by our friends, Schuck and company. If that's the case, we can use any combination of the explosives we have here as breaching material. We lose the element of surprise, but it gets us to medical supplies and food regardless."

The prisoners stood silently, as Waters spoke with clarity and purpose.

"Denise will hopefully not have to transform during our time in the medical bay and can save that as a last resort. There's an extremely high chance that their boutique ammunition designed especially for her is not only better suited for taking her down, it will more than likely fuck us up in ways we can't even imagine. We have some of the same shit, provided what the team down here had wasn't already outdated."

Miller and Marquez glanced over at Denise, who didn't flinch at Waters' suggestion.

"From the med bay, we need to avoid the turrets on the wall. If you can, try to take out the spotlights, but those have reinforced glass around them, same shit they use in personnel carriers these days. It's still possible, but it takes sustained fire to get through. We're going to have to make our way from building to building, tree to tree, using them as cover until we can either get on the walls or we make it to the main gate. Once we get to the main gate, we take the fastest vehicle that can fit all of us and we get the fuck out of here. We don't know whether the boat is even still here, or if they've got those fuckin' hover cabs. Either way, we ought to go to the Jersey side, Philly's too risky."

After a brief moment of silence, Marquez spoke matter-of-factly, "Let's go now, it's as dark as it's going to get out, and we need to use that to our advantage," Marquez began walking towards the access hatch to the maintenance tunnels, with Miller following suit, and Waters, who waved to Denise for her to go before him.

***

Marquez climbed through the narrow entrance to the claustrophobic maintenance tunnels, and landed in a deep puddle with a splash. The remaining prisoners followed suit. The group slowly made their way forward. All that could be heard were their soft footsteps sinking into the softened, damp earth beneath their feet, and the heavy breathing of the anxious prisoners.

Marquez's mind began to race with potentialities of what could be awaiting them at the end of this short but tense journey. Their helmet flashlights lit the hallway, but the heavy concentration of particulate matter in the air created a thick fog that did more harm than good.

"Switch over to night vision, we should be coming up on the debris blocking our path soon," Marquez whispered. Everyone shut off their flashlight except for Denise.

"I don't know how to use this, I'm s-, I'm sorry, what do I do?" Denise whispered back.

"There's a small button next to your right eye, that'll rotate you through vision modes. Press it until you get to night vision, should be two presses."

With two clicks, Denise's flashlight shut off and she could see the hall in a drape of digital blue-green.

After a minute or so more of walking, they came upon the imposing pile of debris. At the top of the debris pile was a small opening, large enough for a young child to get through.

"This is it. We'll watch the rear, Denise you do your thing and let us know when you're ready to move forward again," Marquez said, moving to the back of the procession with Miller and Waters. The three men turned around as Denise began to take her armor off.

The men stood silently, staring into the dark ahead of them. They tried not to jump reactively as Denise's pieces of armor hit the ground.

"Look, I know this is, you know, basically a fuckin' suicide mission, but I have to say, this brings new meaning to getting caught with your pants down," Waters said with a suppressed chuckle.

"Are you fucking kidding me? Now, Waters? Of all fucking times?" Marquez said under his breath, bumping Waters with his shoulder.

"That's it. I'm going to let them kill me," Miller whispered harshly, shaking his head in exasperation. "Only if that joke doesn't do it first."

The thuds of armor hitting the floor stopped, and Denise collapsed to the floor. She fought the urge to scream in pain as her flesh began to squelch, crack, and tear. She had turned into an amorphous form that continued to writhe and contort. Waters and Miller were tempted to look, they wanted to know what could possibly be making those sounds and what it would look like, but they didn't. Marquez already knew that it was painful to watch, and could only imagine how uncomfortable it was for her. While the transformation took only seconds, it felt like an eternity for everyone involved.

The terrifying sounds stopped, and the tip of a tail gracefully lowered in Marquez and Waters' peripheral vision. Out of instinct, they turned around to see what was once the horrifying beast attempting to kill them - only now the beast was using its gigantic claws and maw to move enormous, heavy pieces of debris. Denise took her time and was careful to not drop any of the large pieces of concrete and twisted metal. She placed them on the floor beneath her, making sure to not crush her armor or weapons. A few minutes of thuds and rumbles and the passage was clear. It wasn't perfect, but it was enough that they could get through. She turned her head around at the other three prisoners and let out a low chittering noise.

"Turn around, guys," Marquez said, grabbing Waters and Miller by their shoulders and spinning them around quickly. The three were subjected to the painful sounds of Denise's bestial body reverting back to her human form once again, and Denise was subjected to the overwhelming discomfort that it caused. The sound stopped a moment later, and Miller, assuming the process was over, turned around prematurely.

"Shit! I'm sorry! Fuck, fuck. I forgot about the clothes thing!" Miller yelped out in embarrassment.

"Shhhhhh!" Denise shushed him, "It's fine, but don't tell the whole place where we are!", she scream-whispered. She proceeded to mutter angrily in Chinese under her breath while pulling her gear back on. Miller didn't speak or understand the language, but he picked up on her tone and turned beet-red. Waters did his best not to laugh, while Marquez rolled his eyes.

"Alright, come on," Denise said, the three prisoners turning around slowly and forming back into a line. Marquez took the front with Miller behind him, and they plodded along through the longer stint of the trek.

The lack of soldiers trying to kill them all was welcome, but unsettling. Marquez feared they were being lured into a trap. Had he made his worries known, the other prisoners would have agreed. The journey felt endless as time dilated from looking at the same walls, the same damp floors, the same flora peeking through various cracks in the structure.

"Holy shit, there it is," Marquez whispered, looked back, and gestured the prisoners up to him.

They stared at the ladder, which led up to a hatch that had the thinnest line of white light emanating from its perimeter. They were finally at the medical bay.

"I'll go and see if it's open. Miller, get something ready to use as a door breaching charge, I'm not exactly holding my breath here," Marquez made his way up the ladder, the anticipation grew with each rung. He reached the top and grasped the large handle with his right hand. He sighed deeply and yanked down hard on the handle, which squeaked loudly and echoed in the halls. The subtle sound of the hydraulic latches hissed and Marquez was blinded temporarily as the light of the generator room flooded his night vision. His helmet detected a high-light environment and automatically switched back to standard vision.

Marquez gestured at the other prisoners to come up and set himself up next to the only door in the room, which led to the familiar cloister of the medical bay halls. Miller, Denise, and Waters made it into the room and assumed combat stances with their rifles ready to shoulder at any moment.

Marquez slowly opened the door and slipped into the hallway, checking both directions alongside him. The fluorescent light was a welcome sight to all of them. Denise began to whimper quietly, as this was the first time she had been above the surface in over five years. Marquez waved to the prisoners to head left at the next intersection. He remembered enough of the layout from their break-in to get them going in the right direction.

"Is anyone else finding it strange that no one's here right now?" Miller said quietly as Marquez brought the group into the supply room.

"Grab what you can, aid kits, pills, anything," Marquez didn't answer Miller's question, which angered him.

"Hey, I'm serious. Why the fuck isn't anyone here? Something's not right."

Waters found glucose packs and passed them out to everyone. "Drink up everybody. I know it's not real food, but it's better than nothing."

Miller immediately put his question on the back burner as he tore at the packaging to get the cap off. He, and the others, fervently drank the mushy fruit flavored glucose packs one after another.

"Hey hey, leave a few for later! We're going to crash hard as hell from all of this sugar, and it'll give you a headache that could take down a fuckin' elephant. To your question, they probably took all of the non-combat personnel to the main structure. They knew we were locked down there, so why would they leave them here for us to-"

Before they knew it, they were knocked up against the wall and onto the ground. The sound of the explosion rang in their ears as Marquez scrambled to get back to his feet. Flames and smoke permeated the room as Marquez pulled Miller up from the floor. Denise pulled herself up and grabbed her rifle which had flown some feet away from her. Waters was outside of the room, on top of the door. The explosion must have blown him up against it, and ultimately with it as it left the hinges. The prisoners gathered their weapons and what little of their supplies that they could and went to get Waters.

Marquez and Miller each grabbed one of his arms and lifted him up.

"Water..." he said, pained and panting.

"Yeah, you're Waters. Shit, is he concussed?" Miller said with fear in his voice.

Waters was trying desperately to catch his breath, "No, you fuckin' idiot, water! Look up, it's raining!"

The prisoners looked up at an enormous hole in the building, in which rain was pouring heavily into.

The loud gunfire of the massive turrets penetrated their ears almost as loudly as the building exploding. The prisoners scrambled to find the thickest piece of building remaining to hide behind.

"That fucking asshole knew! Schuck knew this was where we would go!" Marquez yelled angrily, being partially drowned out by the rhythmic gunfire.

"We can use the rain!" Waters shouted over the loud repeating gunfire, as dust and debris flew around them.

"How so?" Marquez shouted back.

"Same reason we couldn't use the fucking flashlights down there. Those spotlights are working against them."

"Okay, so what's the plan?"

"The turrets are spread far enough apart to have some line of sight overlap, but they can't aim straight down. We're going to have to go into the dead zones to move along the wall, but swing out wide back into the heart of the island for when we're back in line of sight."

"If they've got troops on the ground though, we're fucked. Do we have any other options?"

Breathing heavily, Waters shook his head.

***

"Keep firing, don't let them make it out of that building! Fire until I give the order to go in on foot!" Schuck yelled on the radio. He sat, staring intently at an overview of the island and holographic representations of his forces. He had the entire island surrounded by multiple troops. A ringing tone played from the device in the center of the table. Schuck waved his hand over the interface and Wilkins' voice came through.

"What's the situation, Schuck? Right now, I see the whole god damned medical bay in flames."

"Sir, if you recall, it is exactly as I predicted. It was the only logical option for them to take, and they fell for the bait."

"I understand that, but was there any reason to destroy an entire building filled with expensive medical equipment?!"

"Commander, you and I both know that the research on this island holds a thousand times more value than surgical equipment. If we're extremely lucky, the explosion will have killed the prisoners, save for the Manticore. In even the worst-case scenario, it will slow them down and weaken them. We have every single soldier on the wall, they won't get far."

"And if they do?"

"Then we simply make the perimeter smaller. The troops will come down off of the walls and close in until the prisoners are either dead or they've retreated back into the sub levels, in which case we have them back at square one. They're tired and starving. The only one physically capable of going without food for much longer is the Manticore, and the Manticore will have plenty of food after the others have starved to death. We've won, commander."

"I'll believe it when you show me three corpses and the girl."

"Commander, I won't-"

Commander Wilkins cut down the communication, and the topography returned to the holographic projection.

Schuck sat stoically in his chair, not emoting with his face, but seething with rage in his mind. He calmly reached over to the interface and waved his hand over it once again.

"Troops six and nine, cease fire and give me your status," Schuck said trying his hardest to not sound irate.

"Sir, the turrets have reduced the medical bay to rubble, and so far, we haven't seen a single sign of the prisoners. Sir, if I may, I believe they're dead, sir."

"If you haven't seen them, then how can you know they're dead? Take your men and investigate on foot, sergeant. Report to me immediately with anything you find."

***

"They stopped firing. You think they're out of ammo?" Marquez asked, looking at Waters.

"I don't know, but now's our only chance to make our way towards one of the dead zones. Everybody alright?"

Miller nodded and Marquez looked over at Denise.

"I'm fine," She said, looking up at the bright, white moon through the burning, smoldering hole in the roof as the rain pattered on her visor.

"Check your weapons, check your gear, and let's make our way towards the receiving door, remember?"

Waters took the lead this time, with Miller behind him, and Marquez sticking with Denise to make sure she didn't get separated from the group.

The prisoners trod carefully through the smoldering rubble, simultaneously fending off smoke and rain on their visors. The helmets detected a smoky environment and enabled a visual filter that increased visibility. Simultaneously, it detected a wet environment and turned on a defroster which helped evaporate smaller droplets of water.

"Marquez, how's the rear?" Waters asked. He was still looking dead ahead as they approached a burning intersection.

"All clear so far. We almost there?"

"Left at this corner, then immediately on our right."

"Copy that. Miller, Denise, you hear that?"

Miller and Denise responded with a resounding "yes".

The prisoners crept up and over the burnt rubble and turned the corner. Waters checked the remains of an office to his left to see nothing but burning structure. To the right, the receiving vestibule, which was luckily still mostly intact.

"Guess the explosion hit more towards the center of the building," Marquez said observantly.

"That's where I'd hit if I were trying to have the best chance of wiping out majority of the inhabitants," Waters responded out of instinct. He briefly thought about his time back in Stratford with Feig. Shortly after seizing the enemy artillery, he and Feig determined the best targets to hit and where to hit them in order to take out the most enemy soldiers. Their strategically placed artillery strikes alone resulted in 8,000 dead. He hated himself for that and for knowing exactly why Schuck targeted the building the way he did.

"Marquez, check the main door, and do it fucking carefully. We don't know if they've still got people on the wall, and I'd imagine they do. See if you can spot anything," Waters shook off his regrets, he knew he had to stay in the moment.

Marquez carefully stepped over to the window of the man door, very carefully avoiding any obvious lines of sight.

"What do you see?" Waters asked.

"Not much. Rain. Black. That's about it."

Waters rushed over to the window.

"The search lights aren't moving. Their people aren't on the wall, at least not at this particular section. Switch to night vision manually, we're going into the woods. Keep your fuckin' eyes peeled, because there's a very good chance they're out here with us. Widen out a bit in case they use explosives. Ready?"

***

"Troops six and nine, check in," Schuck asked calmly on the communicator.

There was a long silence.

"Squads six and nine, I repeat, check in immediately," Schuck's tone grew slightly annoyed.

Not even static came over the communicator.

***

The prisoners made their way into the woods, fanning out just enough so as not to be one single, easy target. Miller and Marquez were on the far outside of the group, while Denise and Waters were in the middle. They rapidly looked around, searching for human shapes in the digital blue-green blanket of their visors, but had yet to see anything.

Denise heard a twig snap and looked over with her rifle raised to her shoulder, Marquez in a panic waved his hands to let her know that he wasn't a threat. Her heart raced with anxiety and fear. Not only for fear of the soldiers that could be in the same woods she was in but fear of the very real possibility that her inexperience could result in her killing an ally. She heard another twig snap, this time on the right. She saw Waters to her right, who was standing still. Miller was leaning up against a tree and peeked out from it. She heard another footstep. It was loud and clunky on grass and dirt. She saw a soldier a short distance in front of Waters who had now moved behind a tree like Miller. She slowly raised the rifle to her shoulder and flicked the safety off with her thumb. She steadied her trembling. She reminded herself that she knew how to shoot. Waters told her everything he could in a short period of time, and she paid strict attention. One of his lessons stood out in this very moment.

"Don't shoot first unless you absolutely have to," Waters' voice echoed in her mind.

Waters and Miller had both spotted the soldier lazily plodding through the trees and hid flush up against the tree trunks they were standing behind. Marquez saw Denise lower her weapon and stand up against a tree like Miller and Waters. Marquez did the same. Suddenly, there were several more soldiers walking past them all standing stiff up against the trees. Miller bit his lips to stifle the anxiety on his breath.

Waters counted eight soldiers had walked past them. He slowly turned himself and peeked past the tree and saw no more coming. The prisoners looked at each other, their blue-green silhouettes nodding in agreement. They had the clear advantage and now was the time to take it.

The prisoners shouldered their weapons as the soldiers began chit-chatting in the distance. The soldiers had formed a small, tight cluster, just like Waters warned the prisoners about doing themselves, and left themselves vulnerable. Waters took the first shot. In small bursts, the prisoners had slain all eight soldiers in a mere matter of seconds. Waters gestured the prisoners to make their way towards the wall.

Marquez ran over to Denise who was frozen in place.

"Hey, look, you did good, okay? You did good. I saw you when the first one came through. You kept your shit together, you read the situation, and you waited. Now come on, we need to get moving." He tried to assuage her tension of having just killed eight soldiers, but he felt like a hypocrite, having just recently faced his own guilt. He remembered her words, and she listened to his. She released the magazine from her rifle, loaded another one, released the bolt carrier, and ran swiftly towards the wall. Marquez followed behind her, making sure no one was coming from the rear.

The prisoners all arrived at the monolithic face of the wall and leaned up against it. They looked out into the forest for potential enemy soldiers.

"Alright, we're here. The turrets can't hit us here because they can't pivot straight the fuck down. So, we hug the wall until right before the curve of the wall puts us in line of sight of the next set of turrets, then we have to swing back out to the center of the island and back in for the straightaways. Does that make any fuckin' sense? I don't know how else to explain it."

"Yeah, they can aim down, but they have a maximum angle. I tested it out myself when I first got imprisoned here. I tried a few times to see if I could reach the wall, but I was too big of a target, and I was too scared to do it in my normal form," Denise said assertively.

"If you keep this up, you're going to make Marquez and Miller look bad. You guys get the idea?"

"Hug the walls for the straightaways, back out onto the island, avoiding search lights, and Schuck's guys of course, for the curves. Got it," Marquez responded in confirmation.

"Miller? I know you're a little slow on the uptake. You get what we're saying?"

"Fuck you."

"That's a yes. Let's move."

***

The brief static broke the silence in strategic operations, followed by commander Wilkins' booming voice.

"What the fuck is happening on my island, Schuck? You told me you had this under control!"

"It's not over yet sir. Troops six and nine aren't responding, which means most of the prisoners are alive, but the Manticore isn't utilizing its bestial form. It thinks it's going to escape."

"Well, does it think correctly? Because so far all we have are two troops' worth of men whose families we have to lie to about why they're dead! How many construction accidents are we going to have here, Schuck?"

"Commander, if I may be so bold, I don't think you've ever thought beyond the obvious scope of events going on around you. You miss the forest for the trees. Do you understand what's happening, Commander?"

"I don't know who the hell you think you're talking to, but I'll have you dishonorably discharged for disrespecting a superior officer! You little brat, ever since your daddy got you in-"

Schuck waved his hand over the interface on his table and began broadcasting across the entire island.

"Attention all troops, the prisoners have murdered your brothers and sisters in squads six and nine. They have done so in cold blood, despite our multiple pleas for peaceful resolution. Commander Wilkins refused my advice as head of strategic operations when the prisoners first offered to surrender, and is directly responsible for the aforementioned deaths and the current situation. I am hereby taking over the duties of commander for this installation. You are to step onto the island and close in on them. We will not let our brothers and sisters be slaughtered like cattle by traitorous prisoners who should have never even been offered a chance at life for their crimes! Turret

244

operators are to remain in position, you are to shoot to kill, on sight. Troop thirteen, apprehend commander Wilkins to await his trial."

Schuck waved his hand once more and closed the communication channel. Small beads of sweat began to form on his brow.

***

For the first time since they had stepped foot on the island, the forest sounded alive. It was clear that the soldiers were mobilizing en masse, and Waters knew it.

"Shit. I was afraid of this." He said plainly.

"Afraid of what?" Denise asked.

"Those poor fucks we took out a while back haven't checked in with daddy, and thanks to having to take a long, cumbersome route to not become turret fodder, we're not exactly close to the entrance. Schuck just realized we killed his boys, and he knows he still has numbers. He's going to try to overwhelm us."

"What the fuck do you mean 'try'? We were lucky enough to deal with eight without a scratch, let alone a whole fucking company!"

"Denise, I really, really hate to ask you of this, but you know what our only option is here, right?"

Denise nodded and took off her helmet. Without hesitation she took her armor off, throwing it on the ground around her. Waters, Miller, and Marquez formed a wide circle around her, facing outwards to protect her during the transformation process. The vile, painful sounds it made whenever she changed shape didn't sound any better this time around, but the prisoners' adrenaline was pumping hard enough to experience it without trepidation. Fight or flight had kicked in, and flight wasn't an option.

Denise's body bent, grew, and twisted. A few moments later, the hulking form of the Manticore stood among them. Still barely able to comprehend the events unfolding around him, Marquez squeezed out words. "What's next?"

"We try to keep up with her, and we kill every motherfucker that stands in our way. Miller, you've got explosives out the ass, use them. Marquez, you're a good fucking shot, so take out the high priority targets first. Any of theirs that have shit beyond rifles, go for them first."

"And what about you?" Marquez said half-jokingly.

"I'm going to kill the pieces of shit that did this," Waters said with fire in his eyes, before he took off into the forest, with Denise galloping behind him. Marquez and Miller widened out, giving the prisoners as wide of a net as possible.

Waters spotted a small troop tightly packed together about twenty yards ahead of him and Denise. "Miller, you're up!"

Miller armed a concussion grenade and threw it towards the troop. Instinctively, the troop attempted to scatter, but many of them caught in the explosion. Marquez and Waters opened fire, trying desperately to hit the blurry blue-green figures.

Denise noticed another group en route to their position forty yards out. She also noticed a spotlight moving sporadically trying to locate the source of the combat. Denise used her size to her advantage and leapt into the spotlight, drawing its attention on her. The turrets began to fire at the large area where the spotlight was focused. Denise took a bullet to the shoulder, but kept dashing, until eventually she was behind the troop, which the turrets proceeded to rip to shreds. She deftly moved out of sight behind one of the larger trees and stood perfectly still, allowing her wound to heal slowly.

Meanwhile, Marquez, Miller, and Waters fired on the remaining soldiers from the grenade Miller threw. The brief periods of gunfire illuminated the surroundings and interfered with their vision. Luckily for them, it meant that the enemies' vision was being obstructed as well. Miller peeked out from behind a tree and fired a few short bursts towards the enemy soldiers, he hit one of them three times in the chest, which knocked him to the ground, screaming in agony. Marquez followed up immediately after Miller fired, but one of the enemy soldiers had already retaliated against Miller, who took a bullet to the ribs. Marquez killed the shooter with a shot placed perfectly in the visor.

"Miller! You okay?!" Marquez shouted after hiding behind the tree once more.

"I'm okay, he nicked me, but I'm okay. How's Waters?" Miller shouted.

Waters had moved far forward, past the soldiers that Marquez and Miller had just encountered. Waters saw Denise standing still, and he saw the searchlight moving frantically from left to right. Waters prudently hugged up to a tree to avoid being seen by the turrets. The turrets began to fire wildly at random, in the hopes of hitting one of the prisoners. Miller noticed the searchlight and turrets being distracted by something, and he assumed it was Denise. Still bleeding lightly from his wound, he grabbed a few of his explosives and made his way towards the wall. Marquez followed behind him to watch his back. Miller reached the wall and Marquez hid behind a tree while watching for enemy movement from the inside of the island. Miller primed another concussive grenade and tossed it up the wall. His agonizing scream was loud and obvious, but it was quickly drowned out by the cooked explosive he threw up there shortly. The searchlight and turret were engulfed in flames.

"Come on! We gotta keep moving towards the entrance! Pick up the fuckin' pace!" Waters screamed as loud as he could towards the explosion he just witnessed.

Marquez met up with Miller to make sure he was in fighting form, and the two of them proceeded to catch up with Waters and Denise, who had finished healing her wound.

***

"Troops, what is the situation down there!? Respond immediately!" Shuck asked with uncharacteristically obvious anger in his voice.

A cacophony came over the communicator and flooded the room. Some troops were reporting no activity, others were putting through static, gunfire, and screams of fear and pain. One communicator shone through more than the rest. Shuck clenched his fists and gritted his teeth so hard that it caused him significant pain.

He heard the sound of the Manticore roaring and stomping across the island forest floor. He heard the loud, rapid drumbeat of gunfire. He heard the voices of prisoners.

***

Denise and the other prisoners carved through swaths of soldiers, making their way rapidly and aggressively towards the command center. They hoped they would also be making their way towards salvation. They didn't notice the lack of turret fire.

The three prisoners began to lag behind Denise, who was still energetically pouncing and clawing her way through the trees, cutting down soldiers in her way as she went.

"Waters, how are you doing on ammo?" Marquez shouted and panted from exhaustion while leaned up against a tree.

"Not looking too great, but we could be doing far worse. I've scrounged up what I can off the bodies, but we've gotta keep moving!" Waters shouted back with determination in his voice.

"I'm going to come grab a mag. Miller, watch my ass, will you?" Marquez began to trot slowly towards Waters who searched his person for a magazine to give him.

"Miller?" Marquez shouted out again.

"Shit," Waters said plainly. He handed Marquez the magazine and began running over to Miller, who was on the ground in the open. Denise noticed that the other prisoners were lagging behind and turned around to check up on them.

"Miller! You okay? Jesus Christ, get him up. Is he bleeding?" Marquez panicked and with Waters' help, propped Miller up against a tree trunk. Waters gently patted Miller's cheek with the back of his hand in an attempt to get a response out of him. Marquez frantically placed his hands all over his limp body looking for blood or wounds.

"Miller! Snap out of it! Fuck!" Marquez screamed in fear for his friend.

Miller's eyelids opened, revealing a pair of distant eyes. "Let me get one of those sugar packs... I'm crashing, man..." Miller said weakly. Marquez began rummaging through his pockets frantically looking for the glucose packs they managed to take from the medical bay. When he found one, he took the cap off and gave it to Miller immediately, without saying a word. Miller gulped down the sweet, syrupy mush.

Denise caught a glimpse of Schuck's soldiers approaching to the left of the prisoners. She leapt through the trees, weaving in and out of them with incredible agility. The soldiers panicked and began firing blindly, as the fear of the Manticore had stunted their ability to rationalize. She appeared next to them, and her eyes glowed with anger and regret as she raised her large claw and swung it down at the terrified soldiers. Their bodies were rent to ribbons. Denise let out a loud, anguished roar.

"Shit, we need to get going, we're not that far now. C'mon, Miller, on me. Marquez, don't let us get killed," Waters said assertively. He knew they were running out of time. "Come on, Henry, let's go," Waters said as he hoisted Miller's arm up around his neck and shoulders, "Christ, my son Tommy was easier to carry around when he was six for fucks sake. You're like a full-sized toddler, except you're starving to death, yet somehow two hundred pounds heavier."

Denise made her way back to the prisoners and got up on her haunches. She looked around using her superior vision to see if there were any more enemies in the area. She let out a low growl and motioned her head towards the command center. Marquez and Waters began moving, slowly, with Miller on his shoulders. Marquez loaded a new magazine into his rifle, pulled the charging handle, and racked a round. The prisoners began to trek carefully through the woods. Marquez's eyes darted from left to right, and then from right to left. He panned the area as quickly and as often as he could. There was no sign of enemies. Denise trod softly, even softer than the other prisoners whose boots comparatively clunked loudly on the forest floor.

Marquez's heart began to race. The anxiety overwhelmed him as his mind ran through multiple scenarios. Enemies could appear out of nowhere at any moment. Miller was crashing from hunger. Waters was carrying Miller. Denise was powerful and fast, but the specialized ammunition could bring her down if she got hit enough. He wondered what he would say to Wilkins. He wondered what he would say to Schuck. He wondered if he would have the courage to say anything at all. His heart pounded so hard that he could feel it through his armor. He noticed that Denise stopped walking. Marquez looked up to see the familiar gate and the stairs leading up to the command center. He let out a large sigh and closed his eyes.

Chapter 12 - The Land of Rape and Honey

Miller was finally back on his feet again. The sight of the command center invigorated him. Whether it was certain death or salvation, the thought of this ordeal being over one way or another gave him solace. Marquez ripped his helmet off in relief and leaned up against the wall. He thought about how this wall was the very same wall that the three prisoners, plus Feig, had shared a cigarette on mere days before this. Denise made an embarrassed chittering noise.

"I think she wants to change back. You sure? We're not entirely out of this," Marquez asked.

"She'd destroy the stairs and the catwalks if she tried to climb them now, and that's no fuckin' good for anybody," Waters replied.

"What about-" Marquez began, but was cut off.

Waters laughed, "That smug fuck finally got what was coming to him! Look Joey! It's that asshole that was always smiling at us!"

Marquez walked over and recognized the dead man Waters was talking about. The same man that used to smirk and smile at the prisoners laid dead on the ground, with his face frozen in terror.

"Was that you?" Marquez asked as he turned towards Denise.

Denise snorted. Marquez wasn't sure if it was a confirmation or not, but he felt that it was both a confirmation and a scoff.

"Well, either way, you can take his armor. Guys, form a perimeter. Miller, you good?"

"Yeah, yeah, I'm good," Miller responded with renewed energy in his voice.

The prisoners formed a circle around Denise, whose flesh began to morph, break, rip, and tear. The crunching, squelching sounds continued as her skin and bone began to reform into the shape of a familiar human woman. The sounds stopped, and the prisoners all felt the relief of not having to listen to it anymore. They averted their eyes, as Denise walked over to the dead smug soldier and removed his armor piece by piece. She put the pants on first, and then put the top on to make it easier for the men who were steadfastly fighting their basest instincts to peek. Their fight was made a little bit easier by knowing that if she so chose, she could cleave them all to death in seconds.

"Okay, I'm ready," Denise said assertively and without apprehension. "Let's go." She took the rifle from the dead smug soldier and checked the chamber. There was still a round in it and a full magazine.

Marquez nodded and began moving up the stairs. He carefully placed his foot down on every step so as not to make any noise. The other prisoners followed behind him and mimicked his careful steps.

The door was already open. The smoke and din of the destruction around them obscured his vision as he approached the open doorway. With bated breath,

Marquez peeked his head into the command center. He lowered his weapon and slowly entered the office.

"What the fuck, Joey?!" Waters said in an angry whisper.

The prisoners followed Marquez into the command center. The ornate desk stood out in the center of the room, just as it did when they first arrived. The holographic map of the island projected into the middle of the room and illuminated the walls and the subtle geometry of the windows and decorations around the room. The beeps and hums of screens and machines still bounced around the room. Commander Wilkins' head was face down on the desk, with the glow of the screen beneath making his twisted face stand out among the rest of the desk. Blood had spilled over a large portion of the desk, mainly from the exit wound in the left side of his head. A pistol laid on the floor next to his lifeless body, and his right hand was still configured as if it were holding it.

"You've gotta be fucking kidding me! Can't say I'm entirely surprised but Jesus Christ. He knew he lost... Piece of shit took himself out before we could do it," Waters said as rage began to vibrate throughout his very being. "Check the vessel schedule and see if the boat is still here. If it isn't, see if there's something here that can get us to Jersey. Worst case, we fuckin' swim."

"On it. Miller, Denise, keep an eye out, okay?" Marquez asked as he moved Commander Wilkins' lifeless corpse out of the way.

Miller was still recovering from hunger. His mind began to wander as he thought about the foods he wanted to eat. He thought about the restaurants back home in New Jersey that he took for granted for so many years. He thought about being able to sleep in a real bed. Denise looked out at the island from above, in the command center, and began to tear up. As much as she hated this place, she couldn't help but admit to herself the beauty in the trees. She wished she could have seen them under different circumstances.

Three shots fired in rapid succession and Waters screamed out in agony. He turned around, drew his sidearm, and placed a bullet in Schuck's neck. Denise's head snapped to the origin of the sound and her jaw dropped in shock. Marquez ran over to Schuck, who was on the ground in agony, and threw Schuck's weapons across the room. Miller ran over to Waters and began applying pressure to the holes in his torso.

"Fuck, Miller! What the fuck are you doing?!" Waters exclaimed. There was pain and laughter in his voice.

"I'm keeping you alive, dipshit! Joey, is the fucking boat still here?" Miller asked.

Marquez was straddling Schuck, who was laying down on his back with his left hand clutching his bleeding neck. Without a word, Marquez began ferociously beating Schuck's face in with his fists.

"Oh, knock it the fuck off already. Grow up, for Christ's sake," Waters yelled in agony. Marquez stopped. Waters grabbed Miller's hand and pulled it away from his wounds.

"What the fuck, man? You're bleeding out, we need to get you bandaged up!" Miller said angrily at Waters.

"I don't want to get bandaged up, Miller."

"What are you talking about?!"

"I have nothing left!" Waters screamed, "I have nothing. I already lost my wife. I lost my family..." Waters paused, and his face began to twist with tears, "I lost my best fucking friend. There's nothing for me out there..."

"You've got us, man! We may not be nerds and we sure as fuck won't be sleeping with you any time soon, but we're not so bad. Come on, you salty bastard, don't give up now," Miller protested.

Waters laughed as blood began to pour from his wounds, "You guys aren't so bad, but I'm fuckin' tired. I should have been dead years ago... would have at least spared me from this whole fuckin' debacle, but if I wasn't here, who would have babysat your asses? I couldn't have made Denise bear the whole burden," Denise smiled, which caused the tears in the corners of her eyes to sprint down her cheeks.

"This is all your fucking fault you piece of fucking SHIT!" Marquez screamed into Schuck's face. Schuck was in too much pain to reply. Marquez stood up and aimed his rifle at Schuck's head.

"Hey! He's not your kill Joey. He's not your kill..." Waters screamed with all of his energy. "If anyone is going to put that pathetic piece of shit out of our misery, it's Denise."

Denise walked over to Waters who had a devilish grin on his face.

"I'm dying, sweetheart. You know that, right?" Waters asked rhetorically.

"Of course I do," Denise replied with a choked up voice.

"I don't mean to sound dramatic, but if anyone deserves to kill that fucking asshole, it's you. He may have brought us here as cannon fodder, but he... he violated you... and that can't go unpunished."

Denise nodded and smiled.

"Don't get all sentimental on me now. Believe me, you won't forget me. You may have met a few assholes in your life, but none quite like me, I can assure you of that."

Denise laughed, and her laughter shifted into subtle tears. She leaned in to Waters' head and kissed him on the forehead. The tears had run down her face and onto her lips. She tasted the saltiness of her tears on her lips, which only affirmed what was about to happen next.

"It won't bring back what was taken from you, Denise... but it's a start," Waters said lowly into her ear. "And it won't bring back what was taken from us either, but it's better than nothing."

Denise backed away from Waters, who was staring her in the eyes. She walked over to Schuck's pistol that Marquez had thrown away from him and picked it up off of the floor. She pulled the slide back and made sure a round was chambered. Marquez looked over his shoulder and saw her walking over to them with a stoic face. He moved out of the way and looked Schuck directly in the eyes.

Schuck's neck was bleeding badly, and his left hand was covered in blood which was beginning to dry. He opened his mouth as if to speak, and Denise straddled his head, with his own pistol aimed at his face. Without hesitation, she pulled the trigger. Schuck's head was reduced to a pile of viscera and gore, indiscernible from anyone else on the island, save for his uniform. Denise stripped his body and threw his clothing out of the command center in a fit of rage.

Marquez and Miller looked on without a shred of remorse. They knew his end was more than justified, but deep down, they didn't feel it was enough.

"Thank you, Denise. I knew you could do it," Waters said with a smile on his face. "You guys are going to want to get the fuck out of here, because it ain't gonna to get much prettier."

Denise began to cry, because she knew what he meant.

"What do you mean? We're getting out of here, let's go!" Miller said defiantly.

"I already told you, there's nothing for me out there. That asshole is finally dead, which means I got vengeance for Feig. Denise got vengeance for Feig. For all of us. Now get the fuck out of here, I'm not trying to put on a show for all of you. I get stage fright," Waters was laughing and crying all at the same time.

Denise choked back tears and walked towards the door. Miller tried to take off towards Waters, but Marquez grabbed him by the shoulder and pulled him towards the door. The prisoners left the command center, and Marquez closed the door behind him. As the door shut, Waters looked at him and gave him a forehead salute with the pistol in his right hand.

"Denise, are you okay? You're bleeding," Miller asked, as he had noticed that her right side was turning crimson.

"Oh, shit, I didn't even notice," Denise replied, surprised at her own injury.

Miller pulled out some gauze that he had taken from the medical bay and motioned for her to move the armor out of the way so he could bandage her. She lifted the armor and revealed a bloodied ribcage that was partially healed, but oozing blood.

Marquez's adrenaline had finally worn off, and he too noticed a wound that he sustained and didn't realize. The spot between his left shoulder and the side of his neck was bleeding badly and started to feel stiff. He hobbled over to Miller and took a wad of gauze to place on his wound.

*****

Sarah, my love, he thought with laser focus, *I'm sorry I fucked this up so badly.* Waters stared at the gun in his right hand, and he pondered whether he would be able to do what he knew he needed to do. He didn't hesitate because his mind was unwilling, but because his body wouldn't cooperate. He had no choice but to let his mind race and remind him of his children. His mind assaulted him with all of the things he wished he could do and all of the things he wished he could say.

Sarah... Tommy... Chrissy... I love you all. I'm sorry I couldn't protect you. I'm sorry I couldn't save you.

The smile on Waters' face turned into a remorseful grimace. Tears streamed down his cheeks.

Feig... I'm so sorry. You deserved better. You deserved a better friend, and you sure as fuck deserved a better death. I'll see you in hell, pal, he thought and smirked.

His eyes were full of tears, but he didn't have the energy to weep. His sadness quickly turned to anger. He let out a bloodcurdling cry of anguish and hatred.

"Fuck!" he screamed. He began breathing heavily with rage and anticipation. He breathed in sharply, and exhaled a deep breath. He began to slowly, painfully chuckle. "I finally meet some decent people, and this is how you do me?" Waters laughed. "Fuckin' figures," Waters laughed weakly. His memories assaulted him in one final effort to make him change his mind. He remembered what it felt like to feel his wife's lips on his own. He thought about the feeling of his children's arms around his neck. He thought about Feig getting drunk and finally opening up to him after years of avoiding any discussion about the war. He remembered how Feig helped him through his own emotional journey of tackling what he had done, what they had both taken part in. He remembered helping Feig with the same exact thing that one summer night.

With a deep, cathartic sigh, he pulled the trigger.

***

The gunshot was muffled, but the prisoners knew what had happened. Denise whimpered and began to cry shortly after. Miller threw his gun down and shoved his face into his fingers. Marquez wanted to cry to mourn his friend, but he knew he had to get Denise and Miller off of the island first. Despite everything in his mind, heart, and soul telling him otherwise, he rallied himself mentally and emotionally, and matter-of-factly declared their next move.

"We can't linger here. Chances are Schuck notified somebody that the island was compromised, and if we stay here any longer, we run the risk of finding out. We need to get to the docks and get the fuck out of here."

"Is the boat even here? Did you check the vessel schedule?" Miller said through his tears.

"It's still here. We can escape," Marquez went and pulled Miller up with his hand. He then went and grabbed Denise, who was leaning up against the railing of the catwalk. "We need to leave. I know how you feel, but we need to leave."

She hated that he was right, but relented nonetheless.

The prisoners made an all-too-familiar journey back towards the docks they arrived on, and after a few minutes, they found the very same boat that they, in shackles, arrived on. Marquez, Miller, and Denise carefully climbed up the gangway. Their weapons were ready to fend off any resistance, but they found the ship devoid of anyone. The trio meticulously made their way towards the bridge, checking every nook and cranny for a possible hiding soldier. Their journey was quiet, but tense.

"Alright, this is it. Let's get the fuck out of here," Marquez said, noticing the command console in the middle of the room. They were finally at the bridge.

The prisoners were quiet for a few moments.

"None of us know how to drive this thing, Joey. The only person who would have was Feig..."

Marquez punched the console in anger. The numerous switches, knobs, throttles, and holographic interfaces befuddled him, and he knew that they weren't going to be able to take this ship from the island with any sort of confidence.

"So, what the fuck do we do then?!" Marquez yelled in anger.

The prisoners sat in silence for a brief moment. Miller had a stroke of genius, one he wished Waters was here to see.

"Joey, when we were first brought here, do you remember where we were chained up?" Miller asked with excitement.

"Yeah, get to the fucking point Henry!" Marquez snapped.

"There was a lifeboat right next to us, Joey! Those things are *designed* to be easy to drive, because not everyone on the boat is going to be a fucking captain! We can get out of here on that!" Miller said with a growing smile on his face, despite Marquez's anger.

Denise's face bore a tiny, hopeful grin.

Marquez immediately took off running towards the lifeboat, waving on Miller and Denise. Their feet clanged and clunked on the metal deck of the boat until they finally turned the corner and saw the small, red lifeboat.

"Alright, everybody climb in," Marquez said with a strangely calm tone. He twisted the cockpit release switch, which opened up and revealed seats and control console.

"There's only two seats, Joey."

"Denise, are you willing to have a full-grown Italian man sit on your lap for a boat ride to freedom?"

Denise laughed and hopped into the back seat of the lifeboat. Marquez got in the front seat. Denise looked over at Miller and patted her lap, beckoning him to come sit. Miller awkwardly sat on her lap. Denise groaned as if his sitting there was a painful burden.

"Oh my god, are you okay?" Miller said out of reflex.

Denise laughed at him and pulled the cockpit shut over the other prisoners. Marquez waved his hand over the control console which brought up a single option. Marquez couldn't believe how painfully and excruciatingly beautiful the word "launch" was as it was displayed in front of him. He gestured his hand, and shortly after the hydraulic mounts released, and the lifeboat careened swiftly towards the water.

The water sloshed loudly and violently as the lifeboat submerged into the dark, black water of the Delaware river.

Hiding tears of joy, Marquez grabbed the throttle that was clearly marked and slammed it forward.

"We did it... we're free..." he said cathartically.

The lifeboat slowly rumbled its way through the dark water. Marquez couldn't see anything through the viewport, but the holographic projection showed a rough topography of the river. They were barely below the surface, and moving at a meager ten miles per hour, or a little over eight and a half knots, according to the dashboard.

The prisoners sat in anxious silence until the coast appeared on the topographic projection in the front seat. Moments later, the sound of the lifeboat running aground and grinding along the sand and stone permeated the prisoners' ears. Marquez quickly slammed the button to open the cockpit. As the water-tight window was sliding back just above the surface of the water, he climbed out as soon as he could. The lights of civilization filled his view. Miller climbed off of Denise's lap, and she quickly scurried onto land.

"We're in Camden," Marquez said. "We're in fucking Camden, Miller! We made it! We're back in fucking Jersey!" Marquez jumped up and down with joy, as the flames and smoke of Petty Island lingered in the distance.

"We did it, brother, we made it!" Miller added, throwing his arms around Marquez's neck.

Denise slowly walked up to the two and threw her arms around both of their necks.

"What do we do now?" she asked. Her voice carried a mixture of anxiety and despair.

The newly freed prisoners stood on the small, dirty Camden beach for a short while. Miller looked around at them.

"I don't have my helmet, and neither do you Denise," he said, "but Miller has his."

Confused, Miller took his helmet off, and asked, "Yeah, and?"

"Military grade combat gear records all combat data. Biometrics, real-time psych evaluations, positioning, weapon data, ammunition-"

Miller cut him off, "What's your point, Joey?"

"They record audio and visuals, too. They made two years of military service mandatory, so they had to have an insurance policy to make sure that their unwilling soldiers wouldn't lie during after action reviews. We can take the combat data - especially the audio and video of Schuck's crew, of Denise, of everything you saw - and put it out there for everyone to see."

"Joey, we just escaped. We'd be putting a fucking target on our backs!"

"We're already targets. Maybe tomorrow, maybe the day after, maybe a few days from now, someone's going to figure out what happened. Surveillance drones are going to notice the wreckage. Wilkins isn't going to check in with whoever's in charge of him. They'll know we escaped, they'll know *I escaped*, and they'll hunt us to silence us. No matter what," Denise said calmly.

"Feig and Waters died for less. They were just trying to warn people about what was happening right under their noses. For fuck's sake Miller, the rumors we heard about Petty Island were closer to reality than we would have *ever* thought! All that bullshit they were talking in the mess hall. All that bullshit they were on about... they were right. Denise is right, too. They're going to come after us no matter what. The least we can do is put this shit out so they can't silence it."

Miller rubbed his face with his hands, as if to signal his reluctant concession, and brought his helmet over to Marquez.

"We'll put it all on a SecDrive. We'll make copies of that SecDrive, and we'll drop them everywhere we can."

Denise stepped forward between them, and while looking down at the sand beneath her feet, she spoke.

"We're going to make history."

Epilogue

A young man sat in his dimly lit bedroom. The lights and sounds of the suburban night just barely peeked in through the metallic shutters. His eyes were getting heavy as he pored over the information on the screen in front of him. The exhaustion had taken a hold of him, and all of the words combined began to look like gibberish. Defeated, he turned away from the screen to give his eyes a rest.

He moved a stack of SecDrives on his desk out of the way and placed his arms crossed down on the surface. Heavily, he plopped his head onto his crossed arms and let out a long sigh. Each drive had a short descriptor written on it. Some of them were old Federal News Network broadcasts. Others simply had "Misc," Written on them. He was looking for something. A synthetic beep broke the silence he craved.

"Oh, for fucks sake, what is it now?" he said out loud to himself. He stood up slowly from his desk as the beep continued rapidly, urgently. He walked over to an intercom and waved his hand over the interface. "Who is it? What do you want?"

The viewport came on and showed a mysterious figure standing at his front door. The young man didn't recognize who he saw at his apartment door, but whoever they were didn't want to be seen. The shadowy figure left the viewport as quickly as they appeared.

"Wait a minute! Come back!" The young man said just shy of a yell. He darted out of his bedroom towards the door to his apartment. He slowly opened the door and poked his head out of it. Not a single soul was in the hallway. As he closed the door to return to his bedroom, something caught his eye.

"What the-?" he said as his gaze fixated on a small metal rectangle on the floor. He quickly picked up the SecDrive, bolted his door shut and darted back to his bedroom, where he immediately sat back at his display. He mashed a button near a small slot in the desk. "Come on, eject! This fucking thing, I swear to God."

The machine whirred and slowly but surely ejected the SecDrive that was previously inserted. The young man grabbed it and tossed it over by the pile across the way where he was previously trying to rest. With anxious anticipation, he inserted the mysteriously delivered drive waiting to see what was on it.

A myriad of entries populated a list on the display, and shortly after, a video entry began playing.

"My name is Joseph Marquez. What you're about to watch, and even the drive you're watching this on, will make you a criminal in the eyes of your government. If you have no desire to incriminate yourself, then feel free to get rid of it. Give it to someone else, or destroy it. If you want to see how you've been lied to, then keep watching."

Marquez took a long pause. "There's a good chance you'll see my face all around the FedNet. They're going to call us terrorists. Traitors. Criminals.

Enemies of the state. Radicals. What I'm about to show you first is the final testament of a man I had the honor of calling a friend. His name was Philip Waters."

The young man paused the video immediately and pulled picture out from a stack of documents on the left side of the display. The picture showed a young, smiling Waters, holding a toddler boy. On the bottom right of the picture, it read "Tommy, 4".

Thomas' eyes began to well up with tears which he quickly choked back and resumed the video.

"We fuckin' did it. That piece of shit is dead, and that coward Wilkins blew his brains out. I had to watch my wife wither and die, everybody... I'm not alone in that... I lost my kids...." Waters paused, lost in thought. "Joey, Denise, Miller... if you manage to get the fuck out of here, if you can... Find Tommy and Chrissy... if they're still alive, and tell them I'm sorry, and that I love them more than anything in this fucked up world. I'm sorry I couldn't protect them... Fuck! I finally meet some decent people, and this is how you do me? Fuckin' figures..." Waters stared off vacantly. His bloodied, tired face sank into a bittersweet smirk. He closed his eyes, let out a deep sigh, and in the blink of an eye, raised the pistol to his head and pulled the trigger. The force of the bullet caused his now lifeless body to slump over. The footage ended, and Marquez returned to the screen.

"These were the last words of a man who was arrested for the crime of speaking out against a corrupt, oppressive government. Your government. His punishment, like mine, Miller's, and Feig's, was to be death. They hand selected us to go to Petty Island. We were prisoners. What we saw there would sound insane if we tried to tell you," Marquez finished his sentence and Denise entered the scene.

"We have to show you," Denise said stoically, as her body began to crack, break, and shift.

Author's Note

I had no plans to be a writer. I had a few ideas over the years for memoirs of my twenties and how I barely survived them, but I never got very far because, frankly, I don't think anyone else would find my life all that exciting. My desire, or in this instance, *need* to write a complete story out came from a dream I had on April 10th, 2019. In short, the entire story you just read happened in my subconscious, though in dreamland it took place in the past rather than the future. The dream was so vivid and the story riveted me so much that I woke up and entered the synopsis of what would become *Project Manticore* into my phone's memo pad at 4:25am that very morning.

If I were to list every inspirational person that ultimately led to my writing of this novel, I'd have to add about 300 more pages, so I'll give you a short list which is by no means exhaustive:

Robert A. Heinlein for producing what would be my introduction to libertarian science fiction with The Moon is a Harsh Mistress.

Murray N. Rothbard for helping me realize, through his work, that violence and force are unnecessary to order society, and especially that there are no exceptions to this principle. Finally, and most importantly, my wife, who is an avid fiction reader and fellow freedom fighter that gave me honest criticisms on the passages you've just read, and hopefully enjoyed.

I wanted the book to have good pacing. I didn't want to drag on for multiple chapters with what could be conveyed in one, but I also didn't want to move so fast that you didn't have time to process what happened. I used a lot of cinematic devices but transformed them for written word - quick cuts, perspective changes, things that make interesting cinema that I thought could help make interesting literature.

Before I started writing, I read through almost the entire *Witcher* series by Andrzej Sapkowski, and his books are extremely well paced, so I tried my best to mimic that style for the sake of readability. I also wanted to make the dialog realistic. Everyone curses. A lot. Especially in my home state of New Jersey and its surrounding areas. If you paid over $10,000 a year in property taxes, you'd probably be pretty miffed too. The characters are in highly stressful, dangerous, life threatening situations, and while there was a part of me that wanted to dial back the language for some of the more sensitive readers, I couldn't validate having someone like Marquez or Waters say "Dang it! We need to get the heck off of this island!"

Considering this is my first book, and that I have no formal training in fiction writing besides running campaigns in tabletop RPG's, I'm hoping that you enjoyed it and that the amount of time I spent editing, revising, and tweaking was worth it. From start to finish, I have grown immeasurably as a writer, and despite not having any plans to write, I'm glad I dove into it head first. Writing books is easy. Editing them, polishing them, and reaching a point where you, the author, accept them as complete, is not.

That said, I learned to enjoy the process, and I'm proud of what I've created here. I tried very hard to not beat you over the head with moralizing or my philosophy, though they clearly have a large part in the story. I wanted anyone who enjoys science fiction to find something they can resonate with in *Manticore* regardless of their views. With any luck, I succeeded with at least one of my goals in writing this, and if you're here reading this sappy note, then hopefully that means I'm right. At the end of the day, this book is my book, and I never thought I'd have written it, but I'm glad I did.

Thank you, dear reader, it truly means the world. - Ryan A. Bunting

www.ingramcontent.com/pod-product-compliance
Lightning Source LLC
Chambersburg PA
CBHW052037240626
47153CB00006B/2120